Detective Dion: The Silent Blade

DDL Smith

This edition is available to libraries and educational institutions through standard distribution channels.

Published **Worldwide** by **MemoMoo Limited**, London, United Kingdom.

Contents

The Penthouse Mystery

Detective Dion Knight stepped into the penthouse, his tall, athletic frame moving with a fluid grace. The lavish space, a blend of modern elegance and opulent excess, struck him immediately. Floor-to-ceiling windows offered a breathtaking panoramic view of the city, while sleek, minimalist furniture in muted tones of cream and gray filled the expansive living area. Crystal chandeliers hung from the ceiling, casting a soft, shimmering light across the room. Despite the luxurious surroundings, the atmosphere was heavy with the chill of death, drawing all attention to the lifeless body sprawled on the pristine white carpet.

Lydia Harper's lifeless form lay at the center of the room, her once-vibrant eyes now dull and vacant. Her once lustrous blonde hair fanned out around her head like a halo, now dulled and tangled from the events that led to her demise. Her striking features, which had once captured the admiration of many, were now eerily still. High cheekbones and full, perfectly painted lips were frozen in an expression of surprise and horror, a stark contrast to the vibrant personality she had once exuded.

Her elegant, form-fitting evening gown, a deep shade of crimson, clung to her lifeless body, its rich color stark against her pale skin. The gown's delicate fabric was slightly askew, hinting at a brief struggle before her death. Jewelry that once sparkled with life, a diamond necklace and matching earrings, now seemed cold and lifeless, catching the light in a macabre display. Lydia's manicured hands lay palm up, her fingers slightly curled, as if reaching for something that was no longer there. A delicate bracelet on her wrist, with a small silver heart charm, hinted at a more intimate side of her life, now left behind in the silence of the room.

Dion's piercing blue eyes scanned the scene, taking in every detail with meticulous precision. The overturned chair, the shattered glass on the coffee table, and the smudge of red lipstick on a champagne flute told a story of a night that had taken a fatal turn. But what caught his attention most was the knife, gleaming under the overhead lights, its blade clean and free of blood, a perplexing anomaly in the midst of chaos.

The forensic team was already at work, their murmurs blending with the soft hum of the city below. Dion's keen eyes took in every detail, the overturned chair, the shattered glass on the coffee table, and the smudge of red lipstick on a champagne flute. But what caught his attention most was the knife, gleaming under the overhead lights. It lay beside Lydia's body, its blade clean and free of blood, an oddity in the midst of chaos.

Dion knelt beside Lydia, his eyes scanning her still form. There were no obvious signs of a struggle on her body, no defensive wounds that suggested a violent altercation. He leaned closer, his nostrils flaring slightly as he caught the faintest scent of expensive perfume mingling with the cold air. It was then that he noticed the delicate bracelet on her wrist, a charm dangling from it, a small, silver heart. It seemed out of place, too intimate for the impersonal violence that had taken her life.

"Detective Knight," a voice interrupted his thoughts. He looked up to see Officer Stevens, his young partner, standing by with a tablet in hand. Stevens' hazel eyes sparkled with curiosity and a genuine desire to learn, darting around the room as if absorbing every detail with a mix of fascination and determination. His uniform was impeccably maintained, the crisp lines of his shirt and pants a testament to his pride in his role. The polished badge on his chest gleamed under the overhead lights, a symbol of his commitment to the force and his aspirations.

Stevens had always been meticulous about his appearance, understanding that it reflected his dedication and professionalism. His short, neatly trimmed hair and clean-shaven face added to his composed demeanor. At just twenty-seven, he had already gained a reputation for his sharp mind and unwavering integrity. However, it was his ambition that set him apart; Stevens had dreams of climbing the ranks to become a detective, much like Dion.

Dion had seen potential in Stevens early on and had taken him under his wing, guiding him through the complexities of police work. It wasn't just about solving crimes; it was about understanding the human element, reading between the lines, and knowing when to trust your instincts. Dion had become a mentor to Stevens, imparting lessons learned from years on the force, hoping to mold him into a detective who could carry the torch forward.

"We've got the initial reports," Stevens said, his voice steady yet eager. "No signs of forced entry. The door was locked from the inside. The only other way in or out would be through those windows, and we're fifty floors up."

Dion nodded, rising to his feet. "Any witnesses?"

Stevens shook his head. Despite the gravity of the scene, Stevens' perky demeanor was unwavering. He approached his tasks with a youthful vigor, eager to assist and to prove himself. His voice, when he spoke, was clear and enthusiastic, often laced with a note of excitement. There was a sense of idealism about him, a belief that justice could prevail and that he was playing an important part in making it happen. "The neighbors didn't hear anything unusual. The building's security cameras show her entering alone last night. No one else came in or out of her apartment."

Dion's mind raced, piecing together the fragments of the puzzle as he was handed a full statement as to who Lydia Harper was. Her public life made research very easy for the officers. Lydia Harper, a well-known socialite with a penchant for drama, had no shortage of enemies. Her lavish lifestyle and high-profile relationships made her a magnet for both admiration and envy. But who among her circle had the motive and opportunity to kill her?

Lydia had co-owned an exclusive boutique, "Harper & Co.," that catered to the elite of the city. The boutique was not just a store but a social hub where the rich and famous gathered to flaunt their wealth and style. Lydia's keen eye for fashion and her business acumen had turned it into a thriving enterprise, further cementing her status in high society.

Her social calendar was always packed with charity galas, extravagant parties, and exclusive events. Photographs of Lydia, always impeccably dressed, graced the pages of glossy magazines and society columns. Her Instagram account boasted millions of followers, all eager to catch a glimpse of her glamorous life. She was often seen with celebrities, influential politicians, and powerful business moguls, each one vying for her attention and favor.

However, Lydia's public life was not without its shadows. Her success had bred a fair share of rivals, and her personal relationships were often tumultuous. Rumors of bitter feuds with other socialites, strained business partnerships, and a series of high-profile romances and breakups swirled around her. Her latest venture, a luxury lifestyle blog, had sparked whispers of jealousy and sabotage among her peers.

As he pondered this, a man's anguished cry echoed through the penthouse. Dion turned to see Gregory Harper, Lydia's estranged husband, pushing past the police tape. As he entered the penthouse, his demeanor was a volatile mix of grief and rage. His voice, deep and resonant, could shift from a mournful whisper to a booming shout in an instant, reflecting the tumultuous emotions roiling beneath his controlled exterior. Despite the harshness of his presence, there was an air of desperation about Gregory, a man grappling with the tragic loss of his estranged wife and the haunting suspicion that he might somehow be implicated in her death.

"You!" Gregory shouted, pointing a trembling finger at the nearest officer. "You let this happen! How could you let this happen?"

Gregory's eyes, a piercing shade of steel gray, were his most striking feature. They had a hard, cold intensity that could unsettle those who met his gaze. In moments of vulnerability, however, they betrayed a deep well of sorrow and regret, hinting at the complexities of his troubled marriage with Lydia and the burden of his past actions.

Dressed in a tailored suit that spoke of wealth and sophistication, Gregory still managed to exude a sense of disarray. The suit, though expensive, appeared hastily put on, with the tie slightly askew and the top button of his shirt undone. His hands, large and strong, trembled slightly as he ran them through his hair or clenched them into fists, a visible sign of the turmoil within him.

Dion stepped forward, his presence calm and commanding. "Mr. Harper, I understand this is a difficult time, but we need you to stay calm. We're doing everything we can to find out what happened."

Gregory's eyes locked onto Dion's, the raw pain in them momentarily softening. "She didn't deserve this," he whispered, tears streaming down his cheeks. "No matter what happened between us, she didn't deserve to die like this."

Dion nodded, his expression sympathetic but resolute. "We're going to find who did this, Mr. Harper. I promise you that."

As Gregory was led away by another officer, Dion turned back to the scene. His eyes fell once more on the knife, its presence a silent mockery. Someone had placed it there deliberately, a red herring meant to throw off the investigation. But why? And who?

His thoughts were interrupted by a forensic technician who handed him a bagged item, a small, ornate key. "Found this under the couch," the technician said. "Could be nothing, but it might be worth checking out."

Dion took the bag, studying the key with a furrowed brow. Every detail, every clue, was a step closer to the truth. He slipped the key into his pocket, a sense of determination settling over him. This was just the beginning, and he knew that unraveling Lydia Harper's murder would be a test of his skills, his patience, and his resolve.

As he gazed out the window at the sprawling city below, Dion made a silent vow. He would peel back the layers of Lydia's life, uncovering every secret, every lie, until the truth was laid bare. The mystery of the penthouse would not remain unsolved for long.

The news of Lydia Harper's murder spread quickly, casting a spotlight on the penthouse that had once been a symbol of luxury and success. Now, it was the epicenter of a media storm. Reporters and camera crews swarmed the entrance of the high-rise building, their questions and flashing bulbs a constant reminder of the high-profile nature of the case. The public's demand for answers grew louder with each passing hour, intensifying the pressure on Detective Dion Knight to deliver justice swiftly.

Dion stood in the lobby of the building, momentarily away from the crime scene, scrolling through the initial reports on his phone. His mind raced with the details he had observed so far, each piece of evidence a fragment of a larger, more complex puzzle. He felt the weight of the media's gaze, knowing that every move he made was being scrutinized not just by the press, but by a public hungry for answers.

Officer Stevens approached him, his youthful energy undiminished despite the gravity of the situation. "Detective, the initial background checks on the key suspects have come in," he said, handing Dion a folder. "It's not looking pretty."

Dion nodded, taking the folder and flipping through the profiles of the two primary suspects. Both having a connection to Lydia Harper, and each had a potential motive for wanting her silenced.

Gregory Harper: Lydia's estranged husband, Gregory was a wealthy businessman with a reputation for being both ruthless in the boardroom and volatile in his personal life. Their marriage had been a tumultuous one, filled with public spats and private tensions. Recently, Lydia had filed for divorce, which would have cost Gregory a significant portion of his fortune. His history of violent outbursts and the financial strain of the impending divorce made him a prime suspect.

Clara Sullivan: Lydia's best friend and business partner, Clara had been recently embroiled in a bitter dispute with Lydia over a failing business venture. Their friendship had soured, and Lydia had been blackmailing Clara with some incriminating information. Clara's normally composed demeanor had shown signs of cracking in recent weeks, and the stress of the blackmail could have pushed her to a breaking point.

As Dion absorbed the information, the noise from the crowd outside seemed to amplify. He knew the next steps were crucial. Each of these individuals had a motive, and each had something to hide. The task now was to unravel their alibis, decipher their lies, and discover who among them had turned desperation into murder.

"Alright, Stevens," Dion said, closing the folder and slipping it under his arm. "Let's get these interviews started. We need to find out who had the most to gain from Lydia's death, and who had the opportunity to make it happen."

Stevens nodded, his expression resolute. "Yes, sir. I'll set up the interview room."

As they returned to the penthouse, Dion's mind was already crafting strategies for the interviews. He would need to sift through layers of deception, false innocence, and emotional manipulation. The truth was concealed beneath these façades, and Dion was resolute in his mission to uncover it, no matter how deep he had to dig.

While nearing the penthouse door again, a familiar wave of determination surged within him. The media frenzy outside was mere clamor; the true challenge lay in the quiet, precise work of reconstructing a fragmented narrative. Lydia Harper's murder was an enigma waiting to be solved, and Dion Knight was prepared to untangle it, one deliberate step at a time.

As Detective Dion Knight and Officer Stevens made their way back to the penthouse, the elevator doors slid open with a soft chime. They stepped inside, the confined space momentarily offering a brief respite from the chaos of the crime scene above and the clamor of the media below. The elevator ascended smoothly, its soft hum a calming backdrop to Dion's deep contemplation of the tasks ahead.

Just as the elevator reached the 39th floor, the doors slid open to reveal an unexpected visitor, a strange older man in a long, worn coat, his face partially obscured by the brim of a weathered fedora. His appearance was incongruous with the sleek, modern environment of the building. The man's eyes, sharp and intense despite his age, locked onto Dion's with an almost unsettling familiarity.

"Detective Knight," the man said, his voice raspy but urgent. Without waiting for a response, he reached into the folds of his coat and produced a small, folded note. He handed it to Dion, his hand trembling slightly. "This might be of interest to you."

Dion took the note, his curiosity piqued. The man's demeanor and the suddenness of the encounter hinted at something significant. With a curt nod, Dion watched as the man turned and disappeared into the building's corridor, his long coat trailing behind him like a shadow.

As the elevator doors closed once more, rising back up to the penthouse. Dion unfolded the note, scanning its contents. The brief, hastily scrawled message revealed information about Lydia's secret lover, Martin Blake, details that included Martin's troubled past, his strained financial situation, and his deepening desperation. The note hinted at Martin's potential motives and his volatile emotional state, painting a picture of a man who could be driven to drastic measures.

"Looks like we've got a new lead," Dion said, turning to Stevens with a determined look. "Let's add this Martin fellow to the suspect list."

Martin Blake: A struggling artist, Martin was Lydia's secret lover. Their affair had been passionate but fraught with complications. Lydia had promised to leave Gregory and start a new life with Martin, but their relationship was far from perfect. Martin's criminal record, filled with minor offenses, and his unstable financial situation added a layer of desperation to his character. If Lydia had decided to end things with him, Martin might have seen no way out but through violence.

The elevator doors opened once again, and Dion and Stevens stepped out into the corridor, their minds now buzzing with fresh insights as they made their way back to the crime scene. The strange man's cryptic message added a new layer to the investigation, and Dion knew that every clue, no matter how enigmatic, was a piece of the puzzle waiting to be fitted into place.

Dion's mind was already formulating strategies for the interviews. He would need to navigate through layers of deceit, feigned innocence, and emotional manipulation. The truth was buried somewhere beneath these facades, and Dion was determined to uncover it, no matter how deep he had to dig. Each suspect's story was a piece of a puzzle that, when put together correctly, would reveal the complete picture of Lydia Harper's murder.

As Dion approached the penthouse door once more, he felt a familiar surge of determination. The media frenzy outside was just noise; the real challenge lay in the quiet, meticulous work of piecing together a fractured story. Lydia Harper's murder was a high-profile case, drawing public and media scrutiny that could easily distort the pursuit of justice. Dion knew that beyond the flashing cameras and reporters' questions, the truth lay in the careful examination of evidence and the thorough interrogation of those involved.

"Stevens," Dion said with a firm tone, "we need to set up the interviews as quickly as possible. This is turning into a media circus, and we can't afford any delays. The sooner we get to the heart of the matter, the better."

Stevens nodded, his expression reflecting the gravity of the situation. "I've already started making arrangements. We've got Martin and Clara scheduled for later today. Gregory is on standby, depending on how the first two interviews go. I'll make sure everything is set up and ready to go."

Dion admired Stevens' effectiveness. "Good. Keep me informed of any updates. We need to stay ahead of the media frenzy and concentrate solely on the facts. This is a prominent case, and the onus is on us to deliver. Let's ensure our investigation remains thorough and impartial, regardless of the tumult outside."

With their strategy set, Dion and Stevens geared up for a day of rigorous questioning and detailed investigation. Dion understood that solving Lydia Harper's murder would be arduous, but he was ready to confront it with the unwavering resolve and accuracy that had become his trademark. The case was an enigma waiting to be deciphered, and Dion Knight was ready to uncover the truth, one deliberate step at a time.

Three Suspects

Detective Dion Knight entered the interview room, the walls of which were stark and unadorned, a sharp contrast to the opulence of the penthouse. The room was designed for one purpose: to extract the truth. A single table stood in the center, flanked by two chairs, one for the interrogator and one for the interviewee. Dion took his seat, his posture relaxed but attentive, his piercing blue eyes fixed on the door as he awaited the arrival of Gregory Harper.

The sound of footsteps reverberated through the corridor, growing louder until the door swung open. Gregory Harper stepped in, his demeanor a blend of strained composure and barely contained anguish. His tailored suit, though immaculate, seemed to weigh heavily on his shoulders, burdened by more than just fabric. His steel-gray eyes were rimmed with redness, and the deep lines etched into his face spoke of sleepless nights and inner turmoil.

Gregory took a seat across from Dion, his movements deliberate but tense. He ran a hand through his thinning hair, the gesture betraying a flicker of agitation. Dion observed him carefully, noting the way Gregory's gaze flitted around the room, as if searching for a safe harbor in the stark, clinical environment.

"Mr. Harper," Dion began, his voice steady and measured, "I appreciate you coming in to speak with us today. I know this must be an incredibly difficult time for you."

Gregory's eyes met Dion's, his voice a gravelly whisper. "Difficult doesn't begin to cover it. Lydia, she was everything to me, despite what people might think. I, I can't believe she's gone."

Dion nodded, maintaining a calm and neutral expression. "I understand. I need to ask you some questions about your relationship with Lydia and your whereabouts last night. Can you start by telling me about the state of your marriage leading up to her death?"

Gregory shifted in his chair, a pained expression crossing his face. "Our marriage had been... complicated. We were in the process of a divorce. Lydia, she wanted to end it all, but I didn't want to give up without a fight. I guess... I guess I was still hoping we could work things out."

Dion took note of the hesitation in Gregory's voice. "And where were you last night, after Lydia left the party?"

Gregory's face tightened. "I was at home, alone. I've got a house on the outskirts of the city. I spent the evening working on some business documents. I didn't leave the house until this morning."

Dion leaned forward slightly, his gaze intent. "Is there anyone who can corroborate your alibi?"

Gregory's jaw clenched, and he shook his head slowly. "I don't have anyone who can vouch for me. My assistant had the night off, and I didn't think to call anyone else. I was... I was preoccupied."

Gregory's eyes darted around the room, the panic beginning to seep into his voice. "Wait, maybe there's someone. I... I ordered takeout that night. The delivery guy, he might remember me. Or, or my neighbor! Mrs. Greene, she might have seen me come home. She's always looking out her window."

Dion maintained his steady gaze, watching Gregory grasp at straws but decided to continue. "Mr. Harper, we've learned that Lydia had been involved in a contentious legal battle with you. The financial terms of the divorce were going to be quite significant. Did this create any tension between you?"

Gregory's face grew darker. "Lydia was intent on making sure I paid for every mistake I made. She was ruthless, and she knew how to hit where it hurt the most. But that doesn't mean I wanted her dead. I wanted to make things right, not... not this."

Dion watched as Gregory's emotions flared, his voice rising in a mix of frustration and desperation. It was clear that Gregory's anger towards Lydia was intertwined with genuine hurt and confusion. Dion took a deep breath, choosing his words carefully.

"I need to ask you about your interactions with Lydia in the days leading up to her death. Did you have any recent confrontations or discussions with her?"

Gregory's eyes narrowed, his gaze intense. "We had a few arguments, yes. But nothing out of the ordinary. I tried to reach her last night, but she didn't answer. I didn't know anything was wrong until I received the call from the police."

Dion scrutinized Gregory's face for any hint of deceit, but his expression remained one of sincere distress. "We've also discovered that Lydia had a secret lover. Are you aware of this?"

The mention of the affair made Gregory flinch, a shadow of anger flickering in his eyes. "I know she was seeing someone after we split. She wouldn't tell me who. I wasn't happy about it, but I never imagined it would lead to something like this."

Dion nodded, his mind already turning over the new information. "Thank you for your time, Mr. Harper. We may have more questions for you as the investigation progresses."

Gregory stood up, his movements slow and heavy. "I just want this nightmare to end. Please find out who did this to her."

As Gregory left the room, Dion sat in silence for a moment, reflecting on the interview. The man's emotional turmoil and partial admissions added complexity to the case. Gregory Harper was clearly troubled, but whether he was a victim of circumstance or a man with hidden motives was yet to be determined.

Dion glanced at the folder containing the profiles of the other suspects. Martin Blake and Clara Sullivan were next, and Dion knew that understanding their perspectives would be crucial in unraveling the truth behind Lydia Harper's murder. The investigation was only beginning, and each interview was a step closer to uncovering the full story.

The door to the interview room opened again, and Martin Blake stepped in, a clear contrast to Gregory Harper. The artist's presence was a marked departure from the high tension of the previous interview. Clad in a threadbare charcoal-gray sweater and jeans, Martin's attire reflected his worn and troubled expression. Despite his youthful features, his face showed telltale signs of stress and sleepless nights.

Martin took a seat across from Detective Dion Knight, his movements hesitant but defiant. His dark brown eyes, once vibrant and full of dreams, now looked tired and wary. His hair, a tousled mess of curls, seemed to mirror the chaotic state of his mind. He clasped his hands tightly on the table, the knuckles white from the pressure.

"Mr. Blake," Dion began, his voice calm and authoritative, "thank you for coming in. I know this is a difficult situation for you."

Martin glanced up, his eyes reflecting a mix of anguish and defiance. "Difficult doesn't even start to cover it. Lydia's dead, and they think I had something to do with it. I, I loved her, Detective. I'd never hurt her."

Dion nodded, noting the tension in Martin's voice. "I understand. I need to ask you about your relationship with Lydia. When did it start, and how serious was it?"

Martin swallowed hard, his gaze dropping to the table. "We met about a year ago. It started as just an affair, something... something to take our minds off our troubles. But it grew into something real. We talked about a future together, leaving everything behind, starting fresh. But lately, things weren't going so well. Lydia was... distant."

Dion observed Martin carefully, watching for any signs of deceit. "You mentioned that Lydia was distant. Can you elaborate on what you mean by that? Did you have any recent disagreements?"

Martin's face clouded with pain. "She'd been pulling away for weeks. She said she was having doubts about leaving Gregory and starting a new life with me. It was like she was changing her mind, and I couldn't understand why. We had a fight the night before she died. I, " Martin's voice cracked, and he paused to regain his composure. "I begged her to be honest with me."

Dion leaned forward slightly. "Where were you last night, after your argument with Lydia?"

Martin looked up, a hint of desperation in his eyes. "I went back to my studio. I've got an old warehouse down by the docks where I work. I was there all night, trying to finish a piece. I didn't leave until this morning."

"Can anyone vouch for your whereabouts?" Dion asked.

Martin shook his head. "Not really. I'm usually alone when I work. I didn't expect to need anyone to confirm where I was. I didn't think... I didn't think this would happen."

Dion noted the unease in Martin's voice. "We've also come across some information about your financial situation. It seems you've been struggling recently. Could this have played a role in your relationship with Lydia?"

Martin's face flushed with embarrassment. "Yeah, I've been having a rough time. I was behind on rent, and my work wasn't selling. Lydia knew about it, and she tried to help me out, but I hated feeling like a burden. It put a strain on us, but I never wanted her to end up dead because of it."

Dion's gaze was steady, trying to gauge the truth in Martin's responses. "And what about the note I received? It mentioned your affair with Lydia and your state of mind. Do you know who might have sent it?"

Martin's eyes widened with confusion and fear. "A note? I don't know anything about that. I was barely hanging on. I didn't even know if Lydia would stay with me, and now, " He trailed off, struggling to hold back his emotions. "Now she's gone, and I don't know why someone would be trying to frame me or make me look worse than I already do."

Dion studied Martin's reaction carefully. The artist's distress seemed genuine, but Dion knew better than to take things at face value. "Thank you for your time, Mr. Blake. We may need to follow up on some of these details as the investigation progresses."

Martin stood up slowly, his movements heavy with the weight of his emotions. "I just want to know who did this to her. She didn't deserve any of this."

As Martin left the room, Dion remained seated, deep in thought. Martin's account was filled with emotional turbulence, but the inconsistencies and gaps left him with more questions than answers. The artist's financial struggles and emotional turmoil added complexity to the investigation, but Dion needed more concrete evidence to determine his involvement.

Detective Dion Knight stepped into the café, leaving behind the cold, sterile police interview rooms and the frenzied reporters outside. The café's interior provided a soothing difference to the chaotic world beyond its doors. Soft ambient light filtered through large windows, casting a warm glow over the space. The walls were adorned with rich, dark wood paneling, complemented by deep green accents that imparted a sense of understated elegance.

Dark wooden tables, each with a smooth, polished finish, were scattered throughout the café. Their surfaces were adorned with small, potted plants, lush ferns and vibrant ivy, that added a touch of nature to the cozy setting. The verdant greenery provided a refreshing pop of color against the darker tones of the wood and the muted earth tones of the upholstery.

Dion approached the counter, where the barista greeted him with a friendly smile. "Good afternoon. What can I get for you?"

"A black coffee, please," Dion replied, his voice weary but polite. He took a moment to glance around, taking in the tranquil atmosphere. The café was quiet, save for the soft hum of background music and the occasional clink of ceramic cups. It was a welcome respite from the intensity of the day's events.

With his coffee in hand, Dion found a seat at one of the tables near a window lit by the midday sun. He sat down, the soft creak of the chair barely noticeable in the serene environment. He placed the steaming cup in front of him, savoring the rich aroma of the coffee as he took his first sip. The warmth of the beverage provided a comforting contrast to the cool air of the café.

Dion leaned back in his chair, allowing himself a few moments of contemplation. The café's peaceful ambiance, a stark juxtaposition to the turmoil of his current investigation, offered him a much-needed pause. The dark wood and lush greenery seemed to cocoon him in a space of calm, allowing his mind to sift through the complex web of interviews and evidence.

Dion's mind churned with possibilities, each suspect's motive and alibi intertwining in a web of deceit and uncertainty. The note mentioning Martin's troubled state was an unsettling development, suggesting that someone was trying to manipulate the investigation. The next interview, with Lydia's best friend and business partner Clara Sullivan, would be crucial in piecing together the remaining fragments of the case.

Returning to the police station, Dion was met with the familiar buzz of activity. The media frenzy had only intensified, a stark backdrop to the gravity of the investigation. He made his way back to the interview room, his thoughts focused on the task at hand.

Clara Sullivan was already seated when Dion entered. Unlike the previous suspects, Clara's presence exuded an air of controlled detachment. She was dressed in a sharp, tailored black suit, her dark hair pulled back into a precise bun. Her demeanor was cold, her eyes, dark and unyielding, held a steely resolve.

"Ms. Sullivan," Dion greeted, taking his seat across from her. "Thank you for meeting with me today."

Clara's gaze met him with a measured, almost clinical focus. "Of course, Detective. I assume this is about Lydia. I'm ready to answer any questions you have."

Dion began, his tone calm but probing. "Let's start with your relationship with Lydia. Can you describe the nature of your friendship and your business partnership?"

Clara's expression remained unchanged, her voice steady. "Lydia and I were best friends and business partners. We started our venture together a few years ago. We had a close working relationship and a personal friendship, but lately, things had become strained."

"Strained how?" Dion asked, noting her impassive demeanor. "We've heard that there were recent disputes between you and Lydia."

Clara's eyes narrowed slightly. "Yes, there were disagreements. Lydia and I had differing visions for the business. She had become increasingly difficult to work with, and her demands were unreasonable. She was also blackmailing me with information I'd rather not discuss."

Dion leaned forward, intrigued. "Blackmail? What kind of information?"

Clara's expression hardened. "I'd prefer not to delve into specifics. Suffice it to say, Lydia used it as leverage to get what she wanted. Our business was failing, and she used her position to squeeze me for more money and control."

Dion noted the tension in her voice. "Where were you last night? Can anyone confirm your whereabouts?"

Clara's gaze was unwavering. "I was at home, alone. I spent the evening working on some documents and planning for the business. My housekeeper can confirm that I was there, but she left early in the evening."

"And what about Lydia's death?" Dion pressed. "How did you react when you found out?"

Clara's demeanor remained cool, almost robotic. "I was shocked and deeply saddened, of course. Lydia and I had our issues, but I never wanted her dead. I'm a businesswoman, not a criminal."

Dion observed her closely. "We've also received information that Lydia had been involved with a secret lover. Did you know about this affair?"

Clara's eyes flashed with a brief, uncharacteristic emotion before she regained her composure. "I was aware that Lydia was seeing someone, but I didn't know who it was. Our relationship was strained enough without adding personal details."

Dion studied Clara's responses carefully. Her coldness and detachment were telling, but they did not necessarily imply guilt. Instead, they suggested a person who was either deeply affected by the situation or skilled at hiding her true emotions.

"Thank you for your cooperation, Ms. Sullivan," Dion said, standing up. "We may need to follow up with additional questions as we continue our investigation."

Clara nodded, her expression unchanged. "I understand. I hope you find out who did this to Lydia."

As Clara left the room, Dion remained seated, reflecting on the interviews. Each suspect had presented a different facet of Lydia's life, but the picture was still incomplete. Gregory's emotional turmoil, Martin's desperate situation, and Clara's cold detachment all added layers to the investigation, but none offered a clear path to the truth.

The case was growing more intricate, and Dion realized he needed to dig deeper into each suspect's background, relationships, and alibis. The upcoming steps would involve verifying their accounts, uncovering additional evidence, and piecing together the puzzle of Lydia Harper's final days.

Shadows of the Past

As evening settled over the city, Detective Dion found himself back at his desk, the remnants of the day's interviews swirling in his mind. The soft hum of the fluorescent lights above cast a gentle glow over the cluttered surface, illuminating the scattered notes and files that chronicled the day's progress. Outside the window, the city lights flickered to life, a vivid contrast to the quiet stillness of the police station. The distant hum of traffic and the occasional siren pierced the otherwise serene atmosphere, underscoring the solitude of Dion's late-night vigil.

Dion leaned back in his chair, his gaze fixed on the jumble of documents and photographs strewn across his desk. Each piece of evidence seemed to blur together, and the weight of the case began to press down on him. He felt a twinge of frustration, his mind racing through the labyrinth of clues, contradictions, and unanswered questions. The more he pondered, the more elusive the truth seemed, as if it was slipping through his fingers like sand.

As Dion sifted through the pile of papers, he turned his attention to Lydia Harper's business dealings. She was a co-owner of a successful fashion company, a position that undoubtedly placed her in the crosshairs of envy and competition. He methodically reviewed her list of business associates, looking for anyone who might have had a grudge. There were several annoyed competitors, businesses that had lost contracts to Lydia's aggressive expansion strategies, but none of them seemed to have a motive strong enough to resort to murder.

He glanced at the celebrity gossip columns, where Lydia's name frequently appeared. She had her fair share of public feuds, most of them with other high-profile socialites and celebrities. A particularly nasty spat with a former business partner had made headlines for weeks, but a closer look revealed that the feud had been settled amicably, at least on the surface.

Dion rubbed his temples, trying to shake off the growing sense of frustration. Every potential lead seemed to fizzle out upon closer inspection. The annoyed competitors had moved on to other ventures, and the celebrity feuds, while sensational, lacked the depth of true animosity. None of them had the kind of motive that would drive someone to commit murder.

He flipped through Lydia's personal files, searching for any hint of a hidden enemy. Her relationships were complicated, but nothing seemed out of the ordinary for someone of her social standing. Friends, lovers, and acquaintances, each had their own story, but none stood out as particularly threatening.

Dion leaned back further in his chair, glancing around at the nearly empty bullpen. Most of the detectives had packed up and left for the day, their departure marking the end of another long shift. The clattering of keyboards and murmured conversations had faded into a soft hush, leaving Dion alone with his thoughts. He knew the routine all too well: finish the day's work, head home, and return refreshed. Yet, for Dion, the idea of leaving the station before feeling completely satisfied with his progress never quite sat right. It was a habit formed from years of pushing through late nights, the belief that answers were often found in the quiet solitude of the office after hours.

As he rifled through the stack of files, Dion's thoughts drifted to the next case waiting on the docket. The paperwork for an upcoming investigation had already begun to accumulate on his desk, a subtle reminder that the cycle of relentless pursuit and resolution was never-ending. His mind started to race through the preliminary details of the new case, trying to piece together what little information he had at this early stage. The thought of diving into another complex investigation provided a distraction from the current case's frustrations.

Officer Stevens entered the room, his footsteps echoing softly in the otherwise silent space. He dropped a file on Dion's desk and sighed, rubbing the back of his neck. "Tough day, huh?" he remarked, glancing at the weary detective. The concern in Stevens' voice was palpable, a reminder of the shared burden they carried.

Dion's shoulders slumped slightly, betraying his exhaustion. "You could say that," he replied, his voice tinged with a hint of frustration. "The more we dig, the more complicated this case becomes. It feels like we're chasing shadows. Every new piece of information seems to add more layers to the mystery instead of unraveling it."

Stevens nodded, pulling up a chair and sitting down. "I've been thinking about the suspects. There's something off about all of them, but nothing that quite fits together. It's like we're missing a crucial piece."

Dion leaned back in his chair, staring at the ceiling for a moment. "It's frustrating. We've got motivations, alibis that don't quite check out, and a lot of conflicting information. But nothing solid enough to make a move."

Stevens sighed again, standing up and stretching. "Well, it's getting late. I'm gonna head out, get some rest. We'll tackle this fresh in the morning."

Dion gave a small nod. "Yeah, you're right. Get some sleep, Stevens. I'll wrap up here and head out soon."

As Stevens walked towards the door, he paused and turned back to Dion. "Don't stay too late, okay? We need you sharp for tomorrow."

"I'll try," Dion replied with a faint smile. "Goodnight, Stevens."

"Goodnight, Detective."

Stevens left the room, the sound of his footsteps fading into the distance. Dion was alone again, the weight of the case pressing heavily on his shoulders. He glanced at the clock on the wall, realizing how late it had become.

He leaned back in his chair, eyes closed, letting the fatigue of the day wash over him. The room was silent except for the occasional rustle of paper or distant murmur of voices in the hallway. This case was proving to be more complex than he had initially thought. Each suspect, each piece of evidence, seemed to intertwine into a web that was difficult to untangle.

As Dion pondered the mystery, his thoughts drifted back to what had first driven him to become a detective. He was just a boy when his father was murdered, an event that forever altered the course of his life.

***

Dion's childhood had been idyllic until that fateful night. His father, Thomas Knight, was a respected investigative journalist, known for his unwavering integrity and dedication to uncovering the truth. Tall and broad-shouldered, Thomas exuded an air of quiet authority. His strong jaw and perpetually furrowed brow were trademarks of his intense focus and determination, while his deep, resonant voice carried a calming assurance that made those around him feel secure. Thomas's presence was both commanding and reassuring, a testament to his professionalism and his ability to connect deeply with people.

At home, Thomas transformed into a figure of warmth and affection. Despite the pressures and long hours of his demanding job, he made every effort to be present for his son. Their home was filled with the comforting sounds of Thomas's laughter and the steady clack of his old typewriter, which Dion had come to associate with safety and comfort. The smell of coffee and the faint scent of ink often lingered in the air as Thomas worked late into the night, his focus shifting from high-profile stories to personal moments shared with Dion.

Thomas's relationship with Dion was marked by an unspoken bond of mutual respect and love. The evenings they spent together were precious to Dion, a time when his father's stern exterior softened into playful banter and tender moments. They would often sit at the kitchen table, Thomas's large, strong hands deftly handling papers while Dion perched on a chair, fascinated by the world his father was uncovering. They shared stories, laughter, and dreams, with Thomas always encouraging Dion's curiosity and nurturing his growing sense of justice.

Thomas often worked late into the night, sifting through stacks of papers and clippings, his old typewriter clacking rhythmically in the kitchen. Young Dion would sit nearby, a curious and bright-eyed child, watching his father with admiration. The sound of the typewriter was a comforting lullaby that accompanied Dion to sleep many nights, a symbol of his father's tireless pursuit of truth.

One night, however, that familiar rhythm stopped abruptly. Dion was jolted awake by the muffled sounds of a struggle downstairs. His heart pounded in his chest as he clutched his blanket tightly, creeping out of bed with a mixture of curiosity and fear. The house, usually filled with the warmth of his father's presence, felt eerily cold and silent.

As Dion reached the bottom of the stairs, a horrifying scene unfolded before his eyes. His father lay on the floor, his once-strong body now lifeless, a pool of blood spreading around him. A shadowy figure, dressed in dark clothes, was rifling through Thomas's belongings, seemingly searching for something specific. The intruder glanced up briefly, their face obscured by a hood, before fleeing into the night, leaving Dion frozen in shock.

The police investigation that followed was brief and inconclusive. Despite Thomas's reputation and the obvious violence of the crime, the case was quickly buried under a mountain of unsolved mysteries. The killer was never found, and the scant evidence collected led to dead ends. Dion's mother, a gentle woman shattered by the loss of her husband, tried to shield her son from the harsh realities of their new life, but the seed of determination had already been planted in Dion's young heart.

In the days and months that followed, Dion changed. The once carefree and inquisitive child became somber and driven. The injustice of his father's death and the lack of closure fueled a burning desire within him to seek the truth. As a teen, the developing passion for justice never stopped; he threw himself into his studies, particularly in areas that would one day help him solve crimes, criminology, psychology, and forensics. The image of his father's lifeless body, the sound of the typewriter replaced by the chilling silence of that night, became the driving force behind his relentless pursuit of justice.

∗∗∗

Opening his eyes, Dion looked around his office. filled with mementos of past cases the team had worked on and the tools of his trade. The determination that had driven him as a child still burned brightly within him, though it had been tempered by years of experience and the harsh realities of the job. He glanced at the files spread out on his desk, the faces of Gregory Harper, Martin Blake, and Clara Sullivan staring back at him from the photographs.

Shaking off the lingering echoes of the past, he refocused on the task at hand. He pulled out the first interviews and photos from the current case, spreading them across his desk. Each piece of evidence, each captured moment, felt like a clue waiting to be connected, a story waiting to be unraveled.

Gathering the files and photographs, Dion moved through the quiet halls of the police station until he found an empty boardroom. Dion entered the boardroom, which was sparsely furnished and hushed, save for the soft hum of the air conditioning. The room had a long, polished wooden table at its center, surrounded by high-backed leather chairs. The walls were adorned with minimalist artwork, but tonight they were about to be transformed into a canvas for the case he was grappling with.

At the far end of the room, a large whiteboard awaited its new purpose. Dion set down his collection of files and photographs on the table and began arranging them with deliberate precision. The whiteboard loomed in front of him, its emptiness now ripe with potential.

He picked up the first photo, a wide-angle shot of Lydia Harper's opulent penthouse, showing the plush interiors and the layout of the rooms. Dion pinned it at the top of the board, marking the scene where everything had begun. Below it, he arranged the close-ups of Lydia's body at the crime scene: the signs of struggle on her clothing, the blood-spattered carpet, the knife that seemed out of place.

Next, he examined the photos of the suspects. Gregory Harper, captured in his once-elegant penthouse, now an image of desperation. Clara Sullivan, her cold, professional demeanor starkly contrasted with the personal turmoil Dion had uncovered. Martin Blake, looking innocent enough but with an air of unspoken tension. Each face was pinned next to a brief summary of their alibis and motives, creating a visual timeline of their involvement.

He paused, his eyes lingering on Martin Blake's photograph. The artist's troubled expression and guarded posture seemed to hint at a deeper story. Dion took a moment to consider if Martin Blake was capable of committing such a crime. This line of thinking was a different turn from the business-minded motives he had been focusing on. Martin was an emotional character, driven by his passions and often ruled by his heart rather than his head. Could those same passions have led him to murder?

Dion tapped his pen against the desk, his mind racing. Martin's relationship with Lydia had been intense and fraught with complexities. There were whispers of a secret love affair, and Martin had known about Gregory's abusive tendencies long before it became public knowledge. The artist had always maintained an aura of innocence, but his familiarity with Lydia's personal life suggested a deeper involvement.

His alibi was shaky at best, and the emotional turmoil he displayed during their interviews hinted at a man on the edge. Dion recalled the way Martin had talked about Lydia, his voice trembling with a mix of reverence and regret. It was clear that she had meant a great deal to him, and the thought of her suffering could have driven him to desperate measures.

He methodically reviewed each piece of evidence as he pinned it up. Stepping back, Dion took a deep breath and surveyed the board. The fluorescent lights of the boardroom created elongated shadows on the walls, with the hum of the air conditioning as his only companion. The room, now filled with a web of photos and notes, felt like a tangible representation of the case's complexity. Dion's eyes grew heavy with fatigue as he reviewed the evidence one last time. The array of images, each meticulously pinned to the board, provided a semblance of order amid the chaos of the investigation.

Realizing that further progress might be hampered by exhaustion, Dion reluctantly decided it was time to call it a night. He took one last look at the board, ensuring that everything was in its place. The pieces of the puzzle were slowly falling into place, but there was still much work ahead. The weight of the case and the lingering thoughts of the day's interviews made it clear that a good night's sleep was essential to tackle the next steps with clarity and focus.

As he gathered his things, Dion allowed himself a moment of quiet reflection. The drive home would give him a chance to clear his mind and recharge. He shut off the lights, plunging the room into darkness except for the dim glow of the desk lamp. With a final glance at the evidence board, he left the boardroom, locking the door behind him. The corridors of the police station felt eerily quiet as he made his way out, the solitude of the late hour contrasting sharply with the bustling activity of the day. Dion knew that tomorrow would bring new challenges, but for now, rest was a welcome necessity.

The Lover's Secret

The following morning at the police station was cloaked in a palpable sense of urgency, the kind that seemed to hang heavily in the air like a dense fog. Detective Dion Knight sat at his desk, immersed in the disarray of notes, case files, and a precarious tower of coffee cups. The dim glow of his desk lamp cast elongated shadows across his face, highlighting the deep lines of concentration and weariness that had settled there over the past few days.

Dion's eyes were tired but focused as he pored over the details of the interviews conducted with Gregory Harper, Martin Blake, and Clara Sullivan. He had spent the night dissecting every word, every nuance of their statements, and the case was slowly starting to coalesce into a clearer picture, albeit one riddled with complications and lingering questions. The threads of the investigation were intertwining, yet the final strands that would weave them all together remained elusive.

His thoughts kept circling back to Martin Blake, the artist who had emerged as a central figure in this labyrinthine case. Martin's emotional volatility, coupled with his financial troubles and the volatile relationship he had with Lydia Harper, made him a person of particular interest. The intensity of Martin's reactions during his interview had been striking, his raw emotional state, combined with a lack of a solid alibi, suggested that he was more deeply entangled in this situation than initially apparent.

Dion was haunted by the sense that this crime had been driven by something far more visceral than mere premeditation. It was shaping up to be a crime of passion, a violent outburst spurred by profound emotional turmoil. The depth of Martin's distress, and his recent personal and financial conflicts, painted a picture of someone who might have been pushed to the brink. His turbulent emotions and unstable demeanor hinted at a potential for volatility that could easily tip into violence.

Determined to explore this line of thought further, Dion knew it was crucial to delve deeper into Martin's world. He needed to confront Martin in his own space, where the artist's environment might offer additional insights into his state of mind and the extent of his involvement. With a resolute breath, Dion gathered his notes and prepared to leave the station. The decision to visit Martin Blake's apartment felt like a necessary step in unearthing the truth, and Dion hoped that the answers he sought might be found in the shadowed corners of Martin's personal life.

As he walked out of the station, the busy morning buzz of the city felt distant compared to the intensity of the task ahead. The sun was just beginning to rise, casting extended silhouettes and bathing the streets in a soft, golden light. Dion's determination was unwavering, the rhythmic click of his heels on the pavement a steady drumbeat of purpose. Every step he took towards Martin's apartment was driven by a mix of tenacity and a deep-seated need to piece together the fragments of this intricate puzzle, hoping that somewhere in Martin's cluttered world lay the key to unraveling the mystery.

Detective Dion Knight drove through the city in his unmarked police car, the hum of the engine a steady companion in the otherwise bustling landscape. The streets were alive with the rhythm of daily life, a vibrant tapestry of activity and motion. Tall skyscrapers loomed overhead, their glass facades catching the sunlight and casting long shadows across the streets below.

The sidewalks were crowded with pedestrians hurrying to their destinations, their conversations merging into a background murmur of urban vitality.

Finally, Dion approached the outskirts of town, where the transition from city bustle to decay was stark. Martin Blake's apartment building came into view, a dilapidated structure that stood out as a relic of a better days long past. The building was a grim testament to neglect, its once-proud exterior marred by peeling paint and broken windows. The brickwork was stained and crumbling, and the iron railings on the fire escapes were rusted and uneven.

Dion parked his car along the side of the road, the vehicle's unmarked nature blending seamlessly with the ordinary surroundings. The street was lined with similar aging buildings, each one showing the wear and tear of time and neglect. Patches of overgrown weeds and litter scattered along the curbs added to the sense of urban decay.

As Dion stepped out of the car, the difference between the vibrant city he had just left and the dilapidated apartment building before him was striking. The hum of the city seemed distant now, replaced by the quieter, more somber ambiance of the neighborhood. The apartment building stood in Desolate relief against the lively pulse of the city, a silent witness to the struggles and stories hidden within its walls.

He knocked on the door of Apartment 3B, and after a moment, he heard the shuffle of footsteps from within. The door creaked open, revealing Martin, who looked disheveled and exhausted. His eyes widened in surprise and apprehension upon seeing Dion.

"Detective Knight," Martin said, stepping aside to let Dion enter. "What brings you here?"

Dion nodded as he stepped into the small, cluttered apartment. The space was dimly lit, with only a few stray beams of light filtering through the grimy windows. Paintings and sketches were scattered around, some framed and some left in disarray.

"I wanted to follow up with you, Mr. Blake," Dion said, surveying the room. "I've been reviewing the details of the case and thought it might be helpful to ask you a few more questions."

Martin led Dion to a small sitting area. As Dion settled into the small, cluttered sitting area of Martin Blake's apartment, his gaze wandered over the scattered art supplies that filled the space. The room was a chaotic blend of creativity and disarray, with paint tubes, brushes, and half-finished canvases strewn about. Amid the haphazard collection of art materials, Dion's eyes were drawn to a peculiar item wedged between a stack of old paintbrushes and an assortment of vibrant tubes of acrylic paint.

There, nestled incongruously among the art supplies, was a knife that bore a notable resemblance to the one found at the crime scene. Its handle, though worn, had a distinctive design, ornate carvings that matched the intricate details of the weapon from Lydia Harper's murder. The blade itself was partially obscured by the clutter but gleamed with a menacing edge, its presence in the artist's workspace sending a chill down Dion's spine. The sight of the knife was a stark reminder of the gravity of the case and raised unsettling questions about its connection to Martin and the violent crime he was entangled in.

Martin gestured for Dion to sit, though the space was so cramped that it felt like an afterthought. Dion took a seat, his gaze scanning the room for anything out of the ordinary.

"Is everything alright?" Martin asked, nervously running a hand through his disheveled hair. "I've already told you everything I know."

Dion fixed him with a steady gaze. "I understand. But there are a few inconsistencies I'd like to clear up. For instance, your alibi for last night. You mentioned working at the studio, but the lack of any corroborating evidence or witnesses is concerning."

Martin's face flushed slightly. "I was alone, Detective. I didn't think I'd need anyone to confirm my whereabouts. I was just trying to get through the night."

Dion nodded, his mind already piecing together the fragments of information. "I also want to talk about your recent interactions with Lydia. You said she was pulling away from you. Did you ever have any conversations about ending the relationship?"

Martin's gaze dropped to the floor. "Yes, we argued. She said she was having doubts, and it was tearing me apart. I tried to convince her to stay, but she was resolute. She said she needed space, but I didn't know it would end like this."

Dion's expression was thoughtful. "There's something else I need to ask you. The note I received mentioned your recent emotional state and financial troubles. Can you explain more about your situation?"

Martin's shoulders slumped. "I've been struggling, yes. My art isn't selling, and I'm behind on rent. I've been under a lot of pressure, and Lydia was one of the few things keeping me going. Losing her... it felt like losing everything."

Dion took in Martin's response, noting the raw emotion and the underlying sense of desperation. It was clear that Martin was deeply affected by the situation, but the extent of his involvement, or whether he was being manipulated, was still uncertain.

"Thank you for your time, Mr. Blake," Dion said, standing up. "I'll need to review some more evidence and possibly speak with you again. Please make sure you're available if we need to follow up."

Martin nodded, his face pale and drawn. "I understand. I just want to know who did this to her."

As Dion left the apartment, he felt the weight of Martin's anguish and the unresolved tension of the investigation. Martin's emotional state and the inconsistencies in his story introduced new complications to the case. The answers Dion sought were still elusive, but he was determined to uncover the truth, no matter how tangled the path might be.

After his unsettling visit to Martin Blake's apartment, Detective Dion Knight returned to the police station, his thoughts heavy with the ramifications of his findings. The image of the knife among the artist's supplies loomed large in his mind, adding another dimension to the case. As he walked through the bustling corridors of the station, the usual din of ringing phones, clacking keyboards, and low conversations mirrored his own heightened necessity.

In the squad room, Dion spotted Officer Stevens at his desk, engrossed in paperwork. The young officer looked up as Dion approached, his face brightening with curiosity. "Hey, Detective Knight. How did it go with Blake? Any new leads?"

Dion sank into a nearby chair, running a hand through his hair. "It was... revealing. Martin's emotional state and financial struggles fit the profile of someone who could be driven to commit a crime of passion. But I found something troubling, there was a knife in his apartment that looks a lot like the one from the crime scene."

Stevens' eyes widened. "That's significant. What's our next move?"

Before Dion could respond, the sharp, authoritative tone of a voice cut through the noise. "Detective Knight, Officer Stevens, Chief Constable's office, now."

Both men looked up to see Sergeant Williams, his expression a mixture of concern and impatience. Dion nodded and stood up, casting one last glance at Stevens before heading down the hall with him. The two officers made their way to the Chief Constable's office, the weight of the case and the mounting pressure palpable in the air.

Upon entering the Chief Constable's office, Dion was greeted by the stern, imposing figure of Chief Constable Harris in his chair. The Chief Constable's office exuded an air of austere authority, its immaculate surfaces and carefully arranged decor reflecting the high standards of its occupant. The room was bathed in a dim, ambient light that cast long shadows across the polished mahogany desk and the rich leather armchair behind it. Despite its meticulous order, there was a certain heaviness to the space, heightened by the smoky haze that lingered in the air. The source of this haze was a delicate elderflower vape, its subtle, floral aroma mingling with the otherwise crisp scent of the room. The smoke swirled lazily around the Chief Constable as he spoke.

"Detective Knight, Officer Stevens," Harris began, his voice clipped and authoritative. "Thank you for coming. Please, have a seat."

Dion and Stevens take their seats as Harris takes a drag of his elderflower vape and coughs it back up. "Elderflower. Who thinks this garbage is up?"

He places the vape on his desk, perfectly aligned next to the paperwork. "I trust you're both aware of the media frenzy surrounding Lydia Harper's murder. The press is in a frenzy, and the public is demanding answers. I need results, and I need them quickly."

Dion nodded, his expression resolute. "We're working on it, Chief. We're following up on leads and piecing together the evidence. The case is complex, and we're making progress."

Harris's gaze was unyielding. "Complex or not, the media spotlight won't wait. I need you to expedite your investigation and bring us a resolution. The public's confidence in our department is at stake, and we can't afford to let this drag on."

Dion felt a knot of tension tighten in his chest. The pressure to deliver results was immense, and the weight of public expectation loomed heavily over the investigation. "Understood, Chief. We'll prioritize the case and work as quickly as possible."

Harris gave a curt nod. "Good. Keep me updated on any developments, and make sure you're on top of every detail. We need to close this case and restore public trust."

With that, Harris dismissed them with a wave of his hand as he picked up his modern cigarette, taking a drag. "Healthier than cigarettes?" He muttered. "Blasphemy!"

Dion and Stevens left the office, the gravity of the Chief Constable's words settling over them like a heavy shroud. Dion thought that at least the Constable was calmed than usual given the intensity of the media attention this case was receiving.

Back in the squad room, the atmosphere was a blend of quiet determination and focused intensity. Dion glanced over at Stevens, who was already deeply engrossed in his task. The young officer's desk was a testament to his organized approach, immaculately arranged with neatly stacked documents on one side and a wireless keyboard and mouse positioned with precision in front of his monitor. A framed photo on his desk caught Dion's eye, a warm snapshot of Stevens' family: his wife, Julia, and their young son, Tommy.

Julia was a striking figure in the photograph, her features soft yet expressive, with gentle green eyes and a smile that conveyed both strength and warmth. Her eyes sparkled with the same kindness that seemed to radiate from her, her long blonde hair framing her face perfectly. Little Tommy, nestled in her arms, had a mischievous grin that suggested a playful spirit. The contrast between Julia's serene demeanor and Tommy's exuberance added a personal touch to the otherwise professional environment, grounding Stevens in the reality of his life outside the precinct.

Dion then turned his attention to his own desk, which presented a stark contrast to Stevens' pristine setup. His desk was a chaotic canvas of case files, photographs, and scattered notes. The wired keyboard and mouse, with their long, tangled cables, lay in a haphazard fashion, evidence of countless hours spent typing and reviewing documents. Stacks of coffee cups, some empty and some half-full, had accumulated at the side, forming an informal but growing monument to his relentless work ethic. The clutter on Dion's desk was not merely disarray; it was a visual representation of the depth of his immersion in the case.

As Dion settled back into his chair, he took a moment to assess the sprawling mess before him. The pressure of the Chief Constable's directive weighed heavily on his shoulders. The case was intricate, with threads of suspicion stretching in multiple directions. While Stevens methodically organized information and pursued leads, Dion grappled with the intricate web of clues and inconsistencies laid out before him. He knew that while the urgency of the investigation demanded swift action, meticulous attention to detail was crucial. Balancing these two imperatives was the key to unraveling the truth and ensuring justice for Lydia Harper. The sense of responsibility was palpable, and Dion's resolve was unwavering as he prepared to dive back into the case, determined to follow every lead and piece together the elusive puzzle.

Dion opened Gregory Harper's financial records and started sifting through the numbers. The sheer volume of transactions was overwhelming at first, but he focused on the most recent ones. The records painted a picture of a man living beyond his means, with significant amounts of money flowing out for luxury goods, expensive dinners, and high-end travel. Gregory's lifestyle had clearly been unsustainable, supported by the substantial wealth Lydia brought into their marriage.

A recent entry caught Dion's eye: a large withdrawal just days before Lydia's death. The amount was enough to raise questions, but without context, it was hard to determine its significance. Dion flagged it for further investigation, noting the need to trace where the money had gone.

As he continued to delve into the financials, Dion noticed another troubling pattern. Gregory's business ventures had been failing, one after another. The divorce proceedings, nearing their final stages, would have left him bankrupt. Lydia's inheritance would have been out of his reach, and he would have been left with nothing but debts and a tarnished reputation.

Dion's mind raced as he considered the possibilities. The financial angle was compelling, but it wasn't enough on its own. He needed more evidence, more context. Was Gregory's motive purely financial, or had personal animosities pushed him to the edge? Had someone else seen an opportunity in Gregory's desperation and framed him?

He scribbled notes furiously, his thoughts coalescing into a plan of action. The next steps would involve looking through the withdrawals. Which bank accounts have been affected.

Stevens approached Dion's desk, sensing his partner's intense focus. "What've you got?"

Dion looked up, his eyes sharp with determination. "Gregory's finances are a mess. The divorce would've left him bankrupt. Now, he inherits Lydia's fortune. We need to dig deeper into this angle. It's starting to look like he had a lot more to lose, and gain, than we initially thought."

Stevens nodded, understanding the gravity of the situation. "I'll start tracing that large withdrawal. See where the money went." Stevens took a deep breath, his youthful determination unwavering. "Let's get to it!"

As they both immersed themselves in their respective tasks, the intricacy of the case continued to unfold. The line between personal vendetta and financial desperation blurred, creating a tangled web that Dion was determined to untangle. The truth was out there, concealed within the details, and he would stop at nothing to uncover it.

A Fractured Friendship

The afternoon sun streamed through the blinds of the police station, casting angled rays, blinding the desks as Detective Dion Knight and Officer Stevens huddled over their research. Papers and files were spread out, interspersed with coffee cups and digital tablets displaying news reports and public records. Their focus was on unraveling the intricacies of Lydia Harper's relationship with Clara Sullivan, spurred by a particularly glaring public fallout that had recently come to light.

Dion sifted through a stack of press clippings and financial reports, each document shedding light on the contentious business deal between Lydia and Clara. The deal in question involved a significant expansion of their mutual business venture, a high-end fashion label that had once been their pride and joy. The expansion was meant to catapult their brand to new heights, involving a major investment in new product lines and a flagship store in an upscale district. However, the deal had been marred by controversy and infighting.

According to the press reports Dion was reading, the public fallout had been both dramatic and highly visible. Clara Sullivan had publicly accused Lydia of mismanaging the funds and making unilateral decisions that jeopardized their business. The clash had been showcased in a series of acrimonious statements and heated press conferences, with Clara alleging that Lydia had diverted crucial capital into personal ventures and neglected the agreed-upon business plans. The media had seized on the scandal, portraying the once-cohesive partnership as a volatile and deteriorating relationship.

The articles detailed the acrimony between Lydia Harper and Clara Sullivan with vivid intensity, painting a portrait of a bitter feud that had captivated both the media and the public. One article, dated a few months prior to Lydia's death, chronicled a particularly explosive incident at a high-profile fashion gala. The event had been a high-stakes affair, attended by a crowd of industry insiders, celebrities, and journalists. In the midst of the glittering crowd, Clara had publicly confronted Lydia, accusing her of financial impropriety in front of flashing cameras and a live audience. The confrontation was captured on film, the footage showing Clara's fiery accusations and Lydia's defensive, flustered retorts. The spectacle had been broadcasted widely, making headlines and drawing attention from media outlets across the country.

The articles painted a dramatic picture of the fallout, describing how Clara's public shaming of Lydia had not only tarnished their professional reputations but had also fueled rampant speculation about deep-seated personal grievances. The rift between the two women was no longer confined to business circles but had seeped into the public consciousness, becoming fodder for gossip columns and television reports. The financial discrepancies between their business dealings, coupled with their public spat, had turned what was initially a business disagreement into a spectacle of personal vendetta.

Dion reviewed the material spread across his desk, pages of newsprint, digital articles, and clipped headlines. Each piece of evidence added layers to the narrative of animosity and betrayal. The files included detailed accounts of their business ventures, marked with red ink and annotations pointing to alleged financial discrepancies. There were reports of Clara's accusations against Lydia for sabotaging deals and mismanaging funds, and Lydia's counterclaims of Clara's unethical practices and attempts to undermine her.

Stevens, working diligently on his tablet, pulled up additional background information on Clara's business dealings. The digital files revealed a complex web of financial transactions and irregularities that hinted at possible motives beyond mere professional rivalry. The data included audit reports, bank statements, and correspondence that detailed questionable transactions and disputed payments. "It looks like this fallout wasn't just about business," Stevens said, his eyes scanning the screen. "There were personal attacks, allegations of sabotage... it seems like things got pretty ugly."

The combination of public humiliation and the failed business venture had clearly left deep scars, both professionally and personally. The files painted a picture of a relationship marred by deceit and betrayal, suggesting that the conflict between Lydia and Clara went far beyond what had been initially apparent.

Dion nodded, his brow furrowing as he considered the implications. "The intensity of their public disputes could suggest a deeper animosity. Clara had the motive of financial ruin and personal betrayal, but the key will be linking this animosity to the night of Lydia's murder. I think we need to ask Clara about her business dealings."

As the afternoon wore on, the sky outside the city's towering skyscrapers shifted to hues of orange and pink, casting a warm sunset glow over the high-rise district. Detective Dion Knight and Officer Stevens navigated through the bustling streets, making their way to Clara Sullivan's sleek, modern office in one of the city's most prestigious buildings. The high-rise office, with its glass façade reflecting the vibrant colors of the setting sun, was a symbol of Clara's success and ambition.

The building's lobby was a study in contemporary elegance, with polished marble floors, minimalist art pieces, and a reception desk that stood as a sentinel to the busy corporate world within. As Dion and Stevens made their way through the lobby, the office space above them was beginning to empty. The usual hum of activity had softened, and the staff were filtering out, leaving behind a quiet, subdued atmosphere.

They ascended to the upper floors, where the fashion business's headquarters occupied a suite of expansive offices. The elevator doors opened to reveal a corridor lined with stylish, high-end furnishings and artfully arranged displays of the latest fashion collections. The setting sun cast a soft, golden light through the floor-to-ceiling windows, adding a dramatic backdrop to the sleek, polished workspace.

At the end of the corridor, they arrived at Clara Sullivan's office, a spacious, well-appointed room with panoramic views of the city. The interior was tastefully decorated, with high-end furniture and elegant décor that spoke of Clara's refined taste and success in the fashion world. Despite the day's end, the office lights were still on, and Clara was visible through the glass walls, seated at her desk, deeply engrossed in her work.

Dion knocked lightly on the door before opening it, his demeanor professional but firm. Clara looked up from her paperwork, her expression a mixture of surprise and guarded composure. Her polished appearance and the efficient ambiance of her office stood in sharp contrast to the tension of their visit.

"Ms. Sullivan," Dion began as he and Stevens entered the office, "thank you for seeing us. We're here to follow up on the recent investigation into Lydia Harper's murder. We need to discuss the public disputes and financial mismanagement that occurred between you and Lydia."

Clara's eyes narrowed slightly, and she set down her pen with deliberate calmness. "Detective Knight, Officer Stevens," she greeted them, her voice controlled and professional. "I assume you're referring to the media circus surrounding our business? I'm not surprised you're here. The fallout from that situation has been quite significant."

Dion nodded, taking a seat across from Clara while Stevens remained standing. "Yes, the fallout has been well-documented. We're particularly interested in understanding the nature of your disputes with Lydia and how the financial mismanagement accusations might have played a role in the events leading up to her death."

Clara's gaze was steady, but there was a flicker of tension in her posture. "The situation was unfortunate. Lydia and I had a professional disagreement about the direction of our company, and it escalated publicly. I accused her of financial mismanagement because she made decisions that I felt were detrimental to our business. But that's all it was, business."

Stevens interjected, his tone probing. "Can you explain how those decisions might have affected you personally or professionally? Was there a point where you felt that Lydia's actions crossed a line?"

Clara's expression hardened slightly. "Lydia's actions didn't just jeopardize our business; they impacted my career and reputation. The public spat wasn't merely about financial issues; it was also about the betrayal of a partnership and the damage to my professional standing. It was deeply personal, but I assure you, I would never resort to violence."

Dion observed Clara carefully, noting the controlled demeanor she maintained despite the evident strain. "You understand that we need to consider all possibilities. The intensity of your public disputes, coupled with the personal and financial stakes, makes you a key figure in our investigation. Can you provide any alibis or witnesses who can verify your whereabouts on the night of Lydia's murder?"

Clara paused, her fingers drumming lightly on the desk. "I was working late that night, preparing for a major presentation. My assistant can confirm my presence here, and I also have security footage from the building's cameras that might show my movements."

Dion nodded, taking note of her response. "We'll need to review that footage and speak with your assistant. It's crucial for us to establish a clear timeline and eliminate any potential connections to the crime."

As the sun dipped below the horizon, the office was bathed in a soft, amber light. Clara's poised facade began to show subtle cracks as the weight of the investigation pressed upon her. Dion and Stevens exchanged a brief, knowing glance, aware that their inquiries were only beginning to peel back the layers of intrigue surrounding Lydia Harper's murder.

With a polite but firm farewell, Dion and Stevens left Clara's office, the quiet of the evening settling over the city. The next steps in their investigation would involve scrutinizing alibis and verifying the details provided, all while navigating the intricate web of personal and professional conflicts that colored the case.

The city was cloaked in twilight as Detective Dion Knight and Officer Stevens made their way to Gregory Harper's new residence. The glitzy glamour of the high-rise district was a distant memory now, replaced by the more subdued atmosphere of a modest apartment complex on the edge of town. The buildings here were older, their facades weathered and their lawns overgrown. The streets were quieter, with the bustling city noise replaced by the occasional murmur of nearby residents and the distant hum of traffic. Streetlamps flickered on, casting a soft, uneven glow over the cracked sidewalks, adding to the neighborhood's somber, almost melancholic feel.

Dion parked their unmarked police car along the street and, with Stevens in tow, approached Gregory's apartment building. The complex was a far cry from the opulence of the penthouse that had been Lydia and Gregory's former home. It was a two-story structure with a weather-beaten exterior, its once-white paint now faded and chipped. The small parking lot was nearly empty, and the only sign of life was the occasional flicker of lights in the windows of the neighboring units.

As they entered the building's lobby, the atmosphere differed greatly from the grandeur of Lydia's high-rise. The lobby was functional but basic, with worn tiles and a few outdated posters on the bulletin board. The air carried a faint mustiness, a reminder of the building's age and the passage of time since its heyday. A dim overhead light flickers intermittently, casting uneven shadows that emphasize the space's utilitarian nature.

Dion and Stevens ascended the narrow staircase to the second floor, their footsteps echoing softly in the quiet hallway. They reached Gregory's apartment, a modest door with a simple brass number plate marking 2B. Dion knocked firmly, and after a moment, the door creaked open.

Gregory Harper stood in the doorway, looking somewhat out of place in his surroundings. His appearance was disheveled, and his eyes bore the marks of sleepless nights and recent stress. The former financier was clad in casual, worn clothing, a stark contrast to the tailored suits he had once been known for. The change from the luxury of the penthouse to this modest apartment was evident in every detail.

"Mr. Harper?" Dion greeted him as he and Stevens entered. "Thank you for seeing us. We're here to follow up on the investigation into Lydia Harper's murder."

Gregory stepped aside to allow them in, his expression a mixture of resignation and apprehension. "Please, come in. I've been expecting you. Things haven't been easy lately."

The apartment was small but clean, with a few pieces of mismatched furniture and personal effects scattered about. The living room, though tidy, had an air of austere simplicity. A threadbare couch and a small coffee table dominated the space, and a modest kitchen area was visible through an open archway. The walls were adorned with a few framed photographs and an old painting that hinted at Gregory's former affluence, now standing as a relic of better times.

Dion and Stevens took seats in the small living room as Gregory settled into an armchair. The disparity between the financier's former lavish lifestyle and his current circumstances was evident, and Dion could sense the weight of the recent upheavals in Gregory's life.

"We're investigating Lydia's murder and need to discuss the recent developments," Dion began. "I understand you've been through quite a lot recently, especially with the divorce proceedings and the change in your living situation."

Gregory nodded, his face showing signs of fatigue and frustration. "Yes, it's been a rough few months. Lydia and I had our disagreements, but this is something I never could have imagined. I still can't believe she's gone."

Stevens glanced around, noting the simplicity of Gregory's new life. "We've been looking into the personal and professional conflicts surrounding Lydia's death. Your recent separation and the ongoing divorce have come up in our investigation. Can you tell us more about the circumstances leading up to the divorce?"

Gregory sighed deeply, rubbing his eyes as if trying to dispel the lingering stress that seemed etched into his features. His face, once full of energy, now bore the marks of sleepless nights and unspoken worries. "The divorce was messy," he began, his voice tinged with exhaustion. "Lydia and I had been drifting apart for a while, and the business troubles only made things worse. We had disagreements about everything, finances, the direction of the company, even our personal lives. It was a series of small cracks that eventually became chasms."

Detective Dion leaned forward, his gaze steady and unyielding. The weight of the investigation hung heavy in the room, and Dion's tone was both calm and probing. "I understand there were accusations of financial mismanagement. Did Lydia ever threaten to take drastic actions or make any statements that might have been seen as a threat or a declaration of intent?"

Gregory's face grew troubled as he considered the question. "Lydia was never one to make threats," he said slowly, his eyes reflecting a mix of sadness and frustration. "But the financial issues did create a lot of animosity. She felt I was undermining her decisions, and I felt she was reckless with our investments. There was tension, yes, but I never thought it would come to this. We fought about everything, from the business to personal matters, but I always believed we would find a way to work through it, even if it meant making compromises."

Stevens, who had been quietly observing, nodded thoughtfully as he absorbed Gregory's words. "Did you have any contact with Lydia on the night of her murder? Any communication or interactions that might be relevant to the case?"

Gregory shook his head slowly, a gesture that seemed to carry the weight of resignation. "No, I didn't," he said, his voice lacking conviction. "We were on strained terms, and I had moved out of the penthouse weeks before. My evenings have been spent trying to get my life back on track, dealing with the fallout of the divorce and my new living arrangements. I wasn't in touch with her that night. I was trying to find some semblance of normalcy, away from the chaos."

Detective Dion's eyes narrowed slightly as he processed Gregory's responses. The tension in the room was palpable, each word carefully weighed and examined. "So, you weren't in contact with Lydia on the night of her death, and you claim to have been focused on getting your life back on track. That's noted," Dion said, making a note in his file. "But we need to be thorough. Can anyone vouch for your whereabouts on that particular night? Any witnesses or records that could confirm your alibi?"

Gregory shifted uncomfortably, his bearing now reflecting a mix of defensiveness and vulnerability. Dion took note of Gregory's responses, his mind piecing together the fragments of information. The financial and personal upheavals, coupled with Gregory's current living conditions, painted a nuanced picture of a man grappling with significant changes.

"Thank you for your time, Mr. Harper," Dion said as he and Stevens prepared to leave. "We'll be following up on the details you've provided and continuing our investigation. If you remember anything else or if there are further developments, please let us know."

Gregory nodded, his expression a mixture of relief and lingering anxiety. As Dion and Stevens left the apartment, the quiet of the evening enveloped them. The sky was painted with hues of deepening twilight, casting a gentle, amber glow over the city's skyline. The hustle and bustle of the city seemed distant here, the noises of cars and distant conversations muted by the soothing backdrop of a cooling summer evening.

Dion and Stevens stepped out onto the sidewalk, the air carrying a faint chill that hinted at the onset of night. The street was lined with trees, their leaves rustling softly in the gentle breeze. Streetlamps flickered to life, casting pools of warm light that contrasted with the dimming sky. The urban landscape, bathed in soft, golden hues, created a noticeable difference from the tension that had filled Gregory's apartment.

As they walked toward their parked car, the reality of their work seemed momentarily suspended in the serene calm of the evening. Dion turned to Stevens, a weary but determined look on his face.

Dion looked over to Stevens, "Pub?"

"Pub."

A Brief Respite

The day had been long and laborious, each hour stretching out like a weary hand as Detective Dion Knight and Officer Stevens navigated the intricacies of Gregory Harper's run-down apartment. Their follow-up interview had been equally grueling, filled with evasive answers and lingering tension. The late afternoon sun was beginning its slow descent, casting long shadows over the city streets.

They needed a break, a moment to step away from the weight of the case and unwind. As they walked through the grittier part of town, Stevens spotted a small, unassuming pub tucked away on a side street. Its sign, faded and chipped, read "The Old Barrel," and the building itself bore the marks of age: long wooden beams, faint yellow paint peeling from the walls, and a weathered charm that hinted at years of stories etched into its timbers.

The old pub exuded a timeless charm that spoke of decades of use and history. The walls were adorned with dark wooden paneling, slightly faded but rich with character. Above the paneling, faded vintage posters and old photographs, yellowed with age, offered glimpses into a bygone era. Some of the frames were crooked, giving the walls a relaxed, lived-in feel.

The floor was made of uneven flagstones that had polished to a glossy sheen over the years. The bar itself, a long stretch of dark mahogany, was beautifully worn from years of use. Its once-shiny surface was now softened by countless elbows and spilled drinks, each mark a testament to the pub's storied past. The barstools, with their sturdy wooden frames and padded leather seats, had a comfortable but worn look, inviting patrons to settle in for a long stay.

Hanging from the ceiling were a few antique lamps, their glow muted by the shades that had gathered dust over time. These lamps cast a warm, amber light that created a cozy, intimate atmosphere. The lighting was low and diffused, casting gentle shadows that added to the pub's rustic charm. In one corner, a small fireplace crackled softly, its warmth contributing to the overall sense of comfort.

The shelves behind the bar were crammed with an impressive array of bottles, each label a reflection of the diverse selection available. The glassware on display was an eclectic mix of old and new, mugs, pint glasses, and tumblers, each with its own unique history. The soft amber light from the shelves made the bottles glimmer, adding a touch of warmth to the otherwise subdued environment.

Scattered throughout the room were a few tables and chairs, their surfaces a mix of dark wood and worn upholstery. The chairs, some with high backs and others with simple, straight lines, were positioned haphazardly, giving the room an unpolished but inviting feel. A few patrons were seated at these tables, engaged in quiet conversation or simply enjoying their drinks, their murmurs blending into a soothing backdrop.

In the corner, a solitary television was mounted high on the wall, its screen displaying muted sports highlights. The sound was turned down, allowing the chatter and clinking of glasses to dominate the auditory landscape. Occasionally, the flicker of the screen added a brief burst of light, momentarily brightening the dimly lit room.

Dion approached the bar first, his tired eyes scanning the limited selection of drinks. "I'll have a dark stout," he said, his voice carrying a note of exhaustion but also a hint of anticipation for the simple pleasure of a good beer.

Stevens, still brimming with a more energetic disposition despite the long day, followed suit. "I'll have a tequila sunrise," he added with a faint smile, his eyes brightening at the prospect of something a bit more cheerful.

As the bartender busied himself with their orders, Dion and Stevens found a quiet corner table near the back of the pub. The table was small but clean, with a couple of mismatched chairs that looked surprisingly comfortable. They settled down, the wooden chair creaking slightly under their weight. Dion's shoulders relaxed for the first time in hours as he took a deep breath, savoring the change of pace from the relentless pace of their investigation.

The bartender soon arrived with their drinks: Dion's dark stout, dark and rich with a creamy head, and Stevens' tequila sunrise, vibrant and refreshing with its layers of color. Dion took a slow, deliberate sip of his stout, letting the deep, roasted flavors wash over him. Stevens, meanwhile, enjoyed the sweet and tangy kick of his tequila sunrise, a small but welcomed departure from the gravity of their day.

As they settled into their drinks and the warm, dim light of the pub, the conversation between Dion and Stevens began to flow more freely. Stevens took a hearty gulp of his tequila sunrise, the tangy citrus flavor brightening his mood.

"So," Stevens began with a grin, his eyes lighting up, "I've got something to look forward to. Julia and I are taking Tommy on a vacation next month. We're heading to the coast for a week. I can't wait. Tommy's been so excited about it, talking about building sandcastles and playing in the waves. He's at that age where everything is an adventure."

Dion managed a faint smile, though his interest seemed more polite than genuine. He nodded in acknowledgment, his mind still partially absorbed in the case they had just worked on. "That sounds nice. A good break is always welcome."

Stevens, clearly thrilled by the prospect of the trip, continued animatedly. "Yeah, it's going to be great. Tommy's been cheekier than ever lately. Just the other day, he told me he was going to build a sandcastle 'bigger than the Empire State Building.' I had to laugh. The kid's got a big imagination."

Dion took another sip of his stout, letting the rich flavors linger on his tongue. "Kids do have a way of keeping things interesting," he said, his voice distant.

Noticing Dion's lack of enthusiasm, Stevens leaned in slightly, his curiosity piqued. "You don't talk much about your family, Dion. Do you have any family yourself?"

"Nope." Dion replied.

"Mum and Dad?"

"Dead."

Stevens raised an eyebrow, sensing there was more beneath the surface. "You don't see them often?"

Dion shrugged, a flicker of something unreadable passing through his eyes. "Not really. I've been focused on my work for as long as I can remember. It's... easier that way."

Stevens took a thoughtful sip of his drink, trying to gauge Dion's mood. "I get that work can take up a lot of your time, but it sounds like you've sacrificed a lot for it. Don't you ever miss having a closer connection with family?"

Dion's gaze drifted to the small window beside their table, where the last rays of sunlight were fading into the evening sky. He took a deep breath, as if weighing the significance of the question. "I suppose. Sometimes. But my work is what keeps me going. It's what I'm good at. It's what gives me purpose."

Stevens nodded, sensing the depth of Dion's dedication and perhaps the loneliness that came with it. "I understand. Everyone finds their own way to cope and stay motivated. I'm just glad we can find moments like this to unwind and share a bit of normalcy."

Dion offered a small, genuine smile this time, appreciating Stevens' attempt to bridge the gap. "Yeah, it's good to have these moments. Even if they're few and far between."

As Stevens finished his drink and waved goodbye, he left Dion alone at the small table. Dion watched him go, the pub's dim light casting long shadows across the empty space. Feeling the weight of the day's work settle on his shoulders, Dion decided to head to the bar for another stout, hoping that the quiet ambiance of the pub might offer a brief respite.

He walked over to the bar and settled onto one of the worn, high stools. The bartender, a grizzled man with a stubbly beard and a weathered face, greeted him with a nod. "Another stout?"

"Yeah, thanks," Dion replied, his voice low.

As the bartender poured the dark beer, Dion glanced around the pub, taking in the faded wallpaper and the mismatched furniture. The TV in the corner, usually tuned to a sports channel or static, was now showing the local news. The volume was turned up just enough for Dion to catch snippets of the broadcast.

The screen displayed images of Lydia Harper's penthouse, with reporters standing outside, speaking into the camera. The news anchor's voice was somber as they recounted the details of Lydia's murder. Dion's attention sharpened as the anchor mentioned Gregory Harper and the ongoing investigation, emphasizing the case's high-profile nature and the intense media scrutiny.

Nearby, two locals sat at the bar, engaged in a low-voiced conversation. One of them, a large man in a long coat, seemed particularly intrigued by the news. His presence was imposing, and he spoke in a gravelly voice that carried over the bar's hum.

"Who do you think did it?" the first local asked, leaning in closer.

The man in the coat took a slow sip of his drink, his eyes fixed on the TV. With a dismissive tone, he replied, "I get paid to help, not to talk about it." His response was curt, and he finished his drink with a practiced nonchalance.

Dion's instincts kicked in immediately. The man's response seemed oddly evasive, and his manner, nonchalant yet guarded, raised Dion's suspicion. The phrase "I get paid to help" echoed in Dion's mind, hinting at a deeper involvement or perhaps a connection to the case that wasn't immediately obvious.

As the man in the coat placed his empty glass on the bar and stood up, Dion's gaze followed him. The man exited the pub briskly, pulling his coat tighter against the chill of the evening. Dion set his glass down, signaling the bartender to keep the tab open, and pushed off the stool.

Without hesitation, Dion slipped out of the pub and onto the street. The man was already several paces ahead, his coat flapping slightly in the breeze. Dion quickened his pace, careful to keep a respectful distance while remaining out of sight.

The street was sparsely illuminated, with the occasional flicker of streetlights casting wavering shadows on the pavement. Dion kept his eyes on the man, who seemed to be heading toward a nearby alleyway. As they turned the corner, Dion slipped into the shadows, attempting to remain as inconspicuous as possible.

The alley was narrow and cluttered with garbage bins and discarded boxes. The man paused briefly, looking around as if ensuring he wasn't followed. Dion pressed against the wall, straining to keep his eyes on the man in the long coat. The alley was dimly lit, its shadows deepening as the evening darkness settled in. The man in the coat reached into his pocket, but before he could retrieve anything, he suddenly froze. His head snapped around, eyes darting to the street behind him. Dion tensed, realizing the man had sensed something.

With a quick, jerky motion, the man pulled back his hand and stuffed it hastily into his coat pocket. His face paled slightly, and he glanced nervously in every direction. Dion held his breath, trying to remain as inconspicuous as possible.

The man's anxiety was palpable. He turned and began to walk briskly, but Dion could see the man's pace quickening into a full sprint as he darted towards the street. His coat flapped wildly behind him, a stark silhouette against the alley's faint light.

Dion's instincts kicked in, and he pushed off the wall, running after the man. But the effects of a few stouts were beginning to take their toll. His legs felt heavy and unresponsive, and despite his best efforts, he couldn't close the gap. The man's footsteps grew fainter, blending with the sounds of distant traffic and the buzz of streetlights.

Frustrated, Dion slowed to a halt, watching as the man vanished into the distance. He leaned against the alley wall, breathing heavily, and scanned the area. The man had disappeared, but Dion's attention was caught by a nearby bar, its neon sign flickering in the twilight. The place looked more lively, with warm, inviting lights spilling out onto the street.

Feeling a mixture of disappointment and curiosity, Dion decided to investigate the bar. He walked over, pushing open the door and stepping inside. The atmosphere was markedly different from the previous pub, lively chatter filled the air, and the clink of glasses and the sound of laughter created a more vibrant ambiance.

The bar was a bustling hub, with people gathered around high tables and the bar itself, engaged in animated conversations. Dion approached the counter and took a seat on a bar stool, signaling to the bartender, who was busy mixing drinks and chatting with patrons.

"Stout, please." Dion said, his voice tinged with fatigue.

The bartender nodded, quickly preparing the drink. Dion surveyed the room as he waited, noting the contrast between the cozy warmth of the bar and the chilly, oppressive atmosphere of the alley. The news channel on the bar's TV was still reporting on Lydia Harper's case, but the volume was turned down low, creating a background murmur rather than an intrusive presence.

A group of locals chatting nearby seemed engrossed in their own theories about Lydia Harper's case, but their discussions were more speculative than substantive. Dion could catch fragments of their conversation, guesses about possible motives, half-formed opinions about the suspects, and the occasional rumor that had circulated through the community. Nothing that seemed to provide new insights or useful leads.

He swirled the pint in his hand, watching the frothy head settle as he took a long, satisfying sip. The stout's deep, roasted flavors were a welcome distraction, a small indulgence in a day that had been filled with relentless scrutiny and pressure. The warmth of the bar and the comfort of the drink began to work their magic, gradually easing the tension that had built up throughout the day.

Dion glanced around the bar, observing the diverse mix of patrons, some engrossed in their own conversations, others quietly enjoying their drinks. The atmosphere was casual and unpretentious, a far cry from the high-stress environment of the police station. It was a reminder of normalcy, a fleeting escape from the intensity of the investigation.

Despite his efforts to relax, Dion couldn't completely shake off the case. His thoughts kept drifting back to the man in the coat and the fleeting glimpse of potential clues that had slipped away. The brief but intriguing encounter earlier had set off a small alarm in his mind, and the man's odd behavior was hard to ignore. Yet, for now, Dion chose to push those thoughts aside and focus on the present moment.

The bartender placed a fresh pint of stout in front of him, and Dion nodded his thanks, taking another sip. The rich flavor and the hum of the bar's ambient noise created a rare sense of peace. Dion allowed himself to unwind, if only for a brief time. The city outside was still bustling, and the night was young, but for now, he was content to simply enjoy the tranquility before the next wave of challenges.

A Staged Clue

The morning light streamed through the police station's windows, illuminating the desks and walls with a golden hue. Detective Dion Knight trudged through the front door, his movements sluggish and unsteady. The previous night's visit to the local pub had left him with a dull headache and the unmistakable feeling of a hangover. He winced slightly as he adjusted his tie, the early hour exacerbating his discomfort.

Officer Stevens, on the other hand, was already at his desk, brimming with energy. His youthful enthusiasm was evident as he greeted Dion with a cheerful wave. "Morning, Detective Knight! Rough night, huh?"

Dion forced a smile, rubbing his temples. "You could say that. I guess I should have taken it easier last night."

Stevens chuckled. "Yeah, I thought you might need a pick-me-up. We've got a busy day ahead. I've been going over the case files and I think I've found a few new angles to explore."

Before Dion could respond, the sudden clatter of footsteps approached their area. A forensic technician, clad in a standard white lab coat and carrying a stack of manila folders, entered the squad room. The technician's face was obscured by the brim of a hat, but the urgency in their steps was unmistakable.

"Detective Knight, Officer Stevens, we need to see you in the boardroom," the technician said, their voice brisk and no-nonsense.

Dion nodded wearily, exchanging a glance with Stevens. The two followed the forensic technician down the corridor to the boardroom, a room dedicated to case briefings and strategy meetings. The walls were lined with whiteboards and bulletin boards, covered in case notes and evidence photographs. A large, polished table dominated the center of the room, with various evidence bags and files neatly arranged around it.

As they settled into their seats, the forensic technician opened a folder and began to present the findings. "We've completed the initial analysis of the evidence collected from the crime scene and the suspect's residence."

Dion leaned forward, trying to focus through his hangover. "What have you found?"

The technician cleared their throat and began detailing the evidence. "First, let's address the fingerprints. We've conducted a thorough examination of the scene and the objects involved. Unfortunately, the fingerprints on most items, including those on the knife, were either smudged or wiped clean. This complicates our ability to identify the true owner of the prints."

Dion's brow furrowed. "What about the knife itself?"

"The knife," the technician continued, "was deliberately planted with Martin Blake's fingerprints. This suggests that the knife was tampered with after the fact. We also found that the knife's handle had been touched in a way that would leave prints, but it seems they were applied with intent to mislead."

Stevens leaned in, clearly intrigued. "So, someone went out of their way to frame Martin?"

The technician nodded. "That appears to be the case. The evidence indicates that while Martin's prints were found on the knife, they were placed there deliberately. We've cross-referenced this with the rest of the crime scene and other evidence collected, and so far, it seems that whoever framed Martin was careful to cover their tracks."

Dion absorbed the information, the implications slowly taking shape in his mind. "So, if Martin's prints were planted, that could mean someone else had a hand in the crime, or at least in setting him up."

The forensic technician nodded in agreement. "Exactly. We're still analyzing other aspects of the scene, but this planted evidence is a crucial piece. It suggests a deliberate attempt to mislead the investigation."

Stevens's eyes sparkled with curiosity. "So, if Martin's prints were planted, what does that tell us about the real perpetrator?"

Dion rubbed his temples, trying to clear the fog of his hangover. "It means we need to shift our focus. The motive and opportunity now need to be reassessed. We might be dealing with someone who wanted to divert attention away from themselves or had a personal vendetta against Martin."

The forensic technician handed over a detailed report and some additional evidence bags for their review. "We'll continue to process the evidence and keep you updated on any new findings."

Dion thanked the technician, who left the boardroom, leaving Dion and Stevens to pore over the new information. The case had just taken a turn that complicated things further but also opened new avenues for investigation.

As Dion reviewed the forensic report, the hangover slowly faded into the background, replaced by a renewed sense of focus. The framing of Martin Blake pointed to a deeper conspiracy, and unraveling it would be crucial to finding Lydia Harper's true killer. The next steps would involve revisiting suspects and evidence with this new perspective, pushing the investigation forward with both caution and determination.

Dion couldn't shake the feeling that something wasn't right. He scrutinized the details of the forensic report, noting every incongruity and oddity. The precise placement of evidence, the meticulous nature of the crime scene, it all felt too orchestrated, too perfect. His mind drifted back to the trial of his first high-profile case, a moment etched into his memory like a scar.

The courtroom had been packed, the air thick with anticipation and tension. He remembered the eyes of the jury, their gazes shifting from the defense to the prosecution, weighing every piece of evidence presented. Dion had been confident, young, and eager to prove himself. The defendant, a prominent businessman, had been accused of a brutal crime, and Dion had worked tirelessly to build a solid case; but brutality hit the accused deeper. Dion had overlooked, jumped to a conclusion that didn't add up. The echoes of the words "Emma Collins has died." raced through his head.

Snapping back to the present, Dion felt a familiar sense of unease. The Lydia Harper case had the same eerie precision, the same potential for hidden truths waiting to unravel. He knew they had to proceed with meticulous care. They couldn't afford any missteps.

"Stevens," Dion said, his voice steady but intense, "Need a coffee?"

Stevens nodded, putting down some paperwork.

The morning chill lingered in the air as Detective Dion Knight and Officer Stevens made their way to the quaint café where Dion had sought solace the previous day. The café, with its cozy, tranquil ambiance, was a welcome reprieve from the harsh realities of the police station. The warm aroma of freshly brewed coffee mingled with the subtle notes of pastries and old books, creating an inviting atmosphere.

Dion and Stevens entered the café, their breath visible in the cool air. The familiar sight of dark wooden tables and lush green plants greeted them. Dion made a beeline for the counter, where he ordered a strong black coffee, a much-needed remedy for his lingering hangover. Stevens opted for a Vanilla oat-milk latte with extra cream, a lighter choice that suited his upbeat mood.

With their drinks in hand, they settled at the same table by the window where Dion had sat before. The sunlight filtered through the café's windows, casting a soft, golden hue over the table and creating a comfortable setting for their discussion. Dion took a grateful sip of his coffee, savoring the rich flavor and the warmth that seeped through his tired body.

"Alright," Dion began, his voice steadying as the coffee began to work its magic. "We've got some intriguing new developments from forensics. The fact that Martin Blake's fingerprints were deliberately planted on the knife is significant. It suggests that someone was trying to frame him."

Stevens nodded, his gaze focused on the window but his mind clearly racing with thoughts. "If Martin's fingerprints were planted, it points to a calculated effort to divert suspicion. The question now is: who benefits the most from framing Martin?"

Dion took another sip, contemplating the significance of the case. "Given the personal and financial stakes, Gregory Harper could be a potential suspect. The affair between Lydia and Martin provides a motive, and Gregory certainly had the motive to retaliate. But there's still a question of whether Gregory knew about the affair before Lydia's death."

Stevens stirred his latte thoughtfully. "The affair would have certainly given Gregory a reason to feel betrayed and seek revenge. But did Gregory even know about the affair?."

Dion set his coffee cup down and leaned forward, his expression serious. "We need to confirm whether Gregory knew about the affair before Lydia's murder. If he did, it strengthens the case against him. If not, we might need to explore other suspects who could have had access to the knife and the opportunity to plant it."

Stevens checked his tablet, where he had noted various aspects of the investigation. "What about the timeline? We should verify if Gregory's alibi during the time of Lydia's murder holds up. If he was indeed out of the area or had a credible witness, it might shift the focus elsewhere."

Dion nodded, his mind already shifting gears. "That's a good point. We should also re-examine any security footage or witness statements that could place Gregory in a different location or confirm his involvement. At the same time, we need to consider other potential suspects who might have known about the affair and had the means to frame Martin."

The conversation was interrupted briefly by the barista, who brought over a fresh croissant as a gesture of goodwill. Dion accepted it with a nod of thanks, appreciating the small comfort. As he took a bite, the taste of the buttery pastry reminded him of the small pleasures that could make even the toughest cases a little more bearable.

Stevens sipped his latte, looking out the window at the bustling street. "The café's a nice change of pace from the police station, but we need to get back to it soon. The case isn't going to solve itself, and if Gregory is our main suspect, we need to move quickly."

Dion agreed, finishing his coffee with a decisive gulp. "Absolutely. We'll need to follow up with Gregory again and push to see if he knew about the affair. There's still a lot to uncover. I'll do that, while you go and try to confirm Gregory's alibi"

As they finished their drinks and prepared to leave, Dion felt a renewed sense of purpose. The case had taken a new direction, and with each step, they were drawing closer to the truth. With their caffeine fix providing a boost, Detective Dion Knight left the café and headed to Gregory Harper's new office in the financial district. The bustling cityscape was a stark contrast to the tranquility of the café, with the high-rise buildings and frenetic activity a reminder of the corporate world Gregory once inhabited.

The sleek, glass-fronted office building was a testament to Gregory's former affluence, though his current office on the lower floors was modest compared to the penthouse he had once enjoyed. Dion made his way through the polished lobby and took the elevator to Gregory's office. The elevator doors opened to a tastefully decorated but comparatively sparse office suite. The walls were adorned with a few framed financial certificates and a large desk dominated the space.

Gregory was seated behind his desk, surrounded by stacks of paperwork and a computer that flickered with graphs and financial statements. The room, while professional, felt somewhat subdued and reflective of the recent changes in Gregory's life. As Dion entered, Gregory looked up from his work, his expression one of fatigue and uncertainty.

"Detective Knight," Gregory greeted, attempting to maintain composure but clearly struggling. "I didn't expect you so soon."

Dion offered a reassuring nod as he approached and took a seat across from Gregory. "Mr. Harper, I need to discuss something crucial with you. We've uncovered new evidence in Lydia's case that suggests someone deliberately framed Martin Blake for her murder."

Gregory's face went pale, and he shifted uneasily in his chair. "The painter? I see. What does this mean for me?"

Dion's gaze was steady, his voice gentle but probing. "The evidence indicates that Martin's fingerprints were planted on the murder weapon. This implies a deliberate attempt to mislead the investigation. We need to understand your connection to this case better. Did you know about the affair between Lydia and Martin before her death?"

Gregory's face paled further, and he looked as though he had been struck by a heavy blow. For a moment, he stared blankly at Dion, his mouth opening and closing as if searching for words. Then, his composure shattered. He buried his face in his hands, the weight of his emotions overcoming him. His shoulders shook with silent sobs, and the room was filled with the palpable sound of his grief.

Dion remained silent, allowing Gregory the space to process his emotions. The sight of Gregory's raw distress spoke volumes. The financial turmoil and the personal betrayal had evidently taken a deep toll.

After a few moments, Gregory's sobs subsided, and he looked up at Dion, his eyes red and swollen. "I didn't know," he managed to say, his voice choking with emotion.

Dion's expression softened with empathy. "So, you had no idea about the affair before Lydia's death?"

Gregory shook his head vigorously, his distress evident. "I swear, I had no idea. I would never have imagined Lydia with someone like that painter! Are you sure it was with him?"

Dion nodded, taking note of Gregory's emotional reaction. "Alright, Mr. Harper. We'll be in touch." As Dion stood to leave, he glanced back at Gregory, who remained slumped in his chair, staring blankly at the desk. The personal anguish Gregory was enduring seemed genuine, but Dion knew that truth was often buried beneath layers of emotion and deception.

Back at the police station, the atmosphere was one of quiet efficiency. Detective Dion Knight entered, his thoughts still consumed by the emotionally charged conversation with Gregory Harper. The hangover had subsided, replaced by a focused resolve to crack the case.

He made his way to the squad room, where Officer Stevens was intently absorbed in reviewing a series of CCTV footage feeds. The dim light of the monitor cast a glow on Stevens's face as he sifted through hours of footage. His demeanor was a mix of determination and curiosity, a stark contrast to Dion's earlier fatigue.

"Hey, Stevens," Dion greeted as he approached the desk. "Any new updates on Gregory's alibi?"

Stevens glanced up, his expression shifting from concentration to relief.

"Actually, yes. I've been reviewing the CCTV footage from the financial district and the surrounding areas for the night of Lydia's murder. Gregory's alibi seems to hold up."

Dion leaned over Stevens's shoulder, scrutinizing the footage displayed on the screen. The feed was timestamped and showed various camera angles of the financial district. "What did you find?"

Stevens clicked through several clips, pausing to highlight key moments. "I tracked Gregory's movements based on the timestamps from his office building's security cameras and nearby street cameras. He left his office around 6:45 PM, which is consistent with his statements. The footage shows him exiting the building and heading toward a nearby parking garage."

The footage shifted to show Gregory entering the parking garage, and the timestamps continued to align with his account. "He was in the garage for about 20 minutes, and then the cameras show him leaving the garage and driving off around 7:05 PM. There's no evidence of him returning to the area until the following morning."

Dion studied the footage carefully, noting the time stamps and Gregory's actions. "What about the rest of his movements? Was there any chance he could have been near Lydia's place during the time of the murder?"

Stevens shook his head. "I cross-referenced the footage with other surveillance cameras in the area. There's no sign of Gregory's car or him anywhere near Lydia's penthouse after he left the financial district. His car was tracked on the freeway, moving away from the city center, which corroborates his statement that he was out of the area."

Dion nodded, processing the information. "So, it looks like Gregory's alibi checks out. He wasn't in the vicinity during the time Lydia was killed."

Stevens agreed, closing the footage and turning his attention back to Dion. We need to look into any additional leads we might have missed.

With Gregory's alibi confirmed, we should look closer at Martin and Clara, especially considering the affair and the financial dispute."

Dion took a deep breath, his mind racing with the next steps in the investigation. "Yes, we need to dig deeper into Martin's and Clara's backgrounds and motivations. The affair might be a key element, but we need more concrete evidence to tie them to the crime or to uncover any other potential suspects."

The Hidden Camera

T he police station's cafeteria offered a brief escape from the relentless pressures of law enforcement, a modest sanctuary where the noise and chaos of the outside world seemed to fade. Its design was no-frills and utilitarian, with long, communal tables that spanned the length of the room. The metal chairs, though sturdy, were worn from years of use, their seats marred by countless scratches and faded patches of fabric. The walls were a patchwork of framed local newspaper clippings, each one capturing notable events and moments of community interest, alongside motivational posters with slogans about teamwork and perseverance. The soft hum of the fluorescent lights overhead created a steady, almost soothing background buzz, blending with the clinking of cutlery and the murmur of subdued conversations.

The air was infused with the mixed aromas of freshly brewed coffee and the day's cafeteria fare. Today's lunch special was a hearty beef stew, a comforting dish that seemed to embody the essence of home-cooked nourishment. The stew was generously ladled onto a simple, chipped plate, its rich, brown gravy mingling with chunks of tender beef and vibrant vegetables like carrots and potatoes. Accompanying it was a slice of crusty bread, its surface golden-brown and slightly crisp, promising a satisfying crunch with each bite.

Detective Dion Knight settled into one of the metal chairs, his posture reflecting the weariness of a long day. He surveyed the modest meal before him, feeling a sense of relief wash over him as he lifted the spoon to his lips. The stew's savory aroma was inviting, its warmth a stark contrast to the chilly air of the police station. Dion took a deep, appreciative breath, letting the scent of the stew mingle with the quiet hum of the cafeteria. With a careful, deliberate motion, he scooped up a spoonful of the stew, savoring the rich, hearty flavors that burst onto his palate. The beef was tender, almost melting in his mouth, while the vegetables added a subtle sweetness and depth to the dish. Each bite was a moment of respite, a brief pause from the relentless focus and intensity of the investigation.

As he ate, Dion allowed himself to relax, the familiar taste of the stew and the comforting presence of the cafeteria offering a temporary reprieve from the weight of the case. The simple pleasure of the meal provided a welcome break, a chance to recharge before diving back into the complexities and demands of his work.

As he was about to take another bite, the sound of footsteps approaching interrupted his moment of reprieve. Officer Miller, an older gentleman who had been with the force for decades, entered the cafeteria, carrying a small DVD case in his hand. He approached Dion's table, his face marked with a hint of urgency.

"Detective Knight," Miller said, his voice steady but laced with the seriousness of his message. "We found something you might want to see."

Dion looked up, his curiosity piqued. He set his spoon down and wiped his hands on a napkin. "What is it?"

Miller placed the DVD case on the table and slid it towards Dion. "This was recovered from a hidden camera at the crime scene. We conducted a deeper investigation at the crime scene and found a false panel in Lydia's bedroom. Behind it, there was a hidden camera. We traced the wires back to a recorder hidden in the closet."

Dion raised an eyebrow, intrigued. "A hidden camera, you say? And

Gregory never mentioned anything about it?"

Miller nodded, his expression serious. "That's right, sir."

Dion went into a state of deep thought. Given that Gregory had lived there, it's odd he never brought it up. Either he didn't know, which seems unlikely, or he's hiding something. The footage on this DVD could be the key to unraveling what really happened that night. Dion leaned back in his chair, tucking the DVD into his jacket pocket. "Thanks for bringing this to me, Miller. I'll review it immediately."

Miller gave a curt nod and walked away, leaving Dion to finish his meal in a distracted manner. The discovery of the hidden camera and its potential contents added a new layer to the investigation. With renewed focus, Dion left the cafeteria, carrying the weight of the investigation's latest twist with him.

He made his way to the nearest empty office, where he could view the DVD in relative privacy. The room was stark and functional, furnished only with a desk and a chair. Dion set up the small laptop on the desk and inserted the DVD, his anticipation palpable.

As the DVD loaded and the video feed began to play, Dion watched intently. The footage was grainy, but it provided a crucial perspective on the events leading up to Lydia Harper's death. The hidden camera had captured movements and interactions that could shed light on the case and perhaps point toward the true perpetrator.

Dion's attention was fixed on the screen, his mind racing to piece together the information as the video unfolded. The footage from the hidden camera was grainy and intermittent, but it provided a crucial window into the last moments of Lydia Harper's life.

The camera had been strategically placed to capture activity in Lydia's living area from the bedroom, but the video was punctuated by unsettling gaps and distortions. At first, the footage showed Lydia moving around her penthouse in what appeared to be a normal evening routine. The graininess of the video made it difficult to discern specific details, but Dion noted the timestamps on the footage, which seemed to align with the time of Lydia's murder.

As the video progressed, Dion noticed several moments of significant interest. Lydia was seen talking to someone off-camera, their face obscured. The conversation was heated, though the audio was too distorted to make out any clear words. The figure was dressed in dark clothing, and their identity remained hidden. The footage then abruptly cut to a different angle, revealing Lydia seemingly alone in her apartment.

But then, the video took an even more alarming turn. There were several brief, jarring interruptions where the screen went black, and the timestamp appeared to jump forward, suggesting that sections of the footage had been deliberately removed or corrupted. The gaps were noticeable, and Dion's frustration grew as he tried to piece together what had been lost.

Just as Dion was about to review the footage again, the office door creaked open. Officer Stevens entered, his face showing a mix of curiosity and concern. "How's it going with the footage?"

Dion gestured to the laptop, his eyes still focused on the screen. "Not as clear as I hoped. There are several interruptions and jumps in the video. It looks like someone tampered with it."

Stevens moved closer, peering over Dion's shoulder at the screen. "Yeah, I see what you mean. These gaps are suspicious. It's almost as if the camera was tampered with to hide certain parts of what happened."

Dion nodded, frustration evident in his voice. "Exactly. There's a lot of missing time here. The footage shows Lydia in what looks like a normal evening, then suddenly there are these unexplained gaps. It's possible that whoever did this wanted to remove specific evidence from the record."

Stevens rubbed his chin thoughtfully. "If we're missing key parts of the video, we need to figure out what was removed. There could be crucial interactions or events that were deliberately erased to mislead us."

Dion leaned back in his chair, deep in thought. "Let's consider what could have been cut out. The conversation Lydia had with the person off-camera could be significant. If that person was a suspect, their interaction with Lydia could provide a motive or a clue about their identity."

Stevens nodded, adding, "And there might have been something in the footage that showed the actual moments leading up to Lydia's death. Maybe the video showed her reacting to a threat or getting attacked. The tampering seems deliberate and aimed at obscuring the truth."

Dion's expression hardened as he considered the implications. "If someone went through the trouble of tampering with the footage, they likely knew we'd find it eventually. It could mean we're dealing with someone who is trying to mislead the investigation or cover their tracks."

Stevens looked concerned. "Do you think this could be an attempt to frame someone or divert suspicion away from the real killer?"

Dion sighed, rubbing his temples. "It's a possibility. We need to be cautious about jumping to conclusions. The tampered footage could indicate a deliberate attempt to set us on the wrong path. We should re-evaluate all our suspects and their alibis in light of this new evidence. We also need to look into how and why the footage was tampered with. It might lead us to the person responsible for the tampering."

Stevens agreed, his mind already racing with possible avenues for investigation. "I'll start by checking if there are any security or maintenance records related to the camera system. There might be a way to track who had access to the system or if any tampering was noted."

Dion nodded, grateful for Stevens's proactive approach. "That sounds like a good plan. In the meantime, I want to see where this camera is. I'm going to go back to the crime scene and try to get an idea of the place." With that, Dion walked out of the room, leaving the investigation from the police side to Officer Stevens.

The apartment, now devoid of forensic teams, felt eerily silent. Dion's footsteps echoed softly on the hardwood floors as he walked to the bedroom. The false wall panel, now exposed, stood out like a glaring anomaly amidst the room's otherwise pristine decor.

Dion aligned himself with the camera's previous angle, envisioning how it had overlooked the main living area through the wide-open doors between the two rooms. The vantage point provided a perfect view of anyone entering or leaving the bedroom. He pondered whether Gregory had known about the camera during his time living there or if it had been installed later, unbeknownst to both him and Lydia. The idea that someone had been secretly watching Lydia, possibly without her knowledge, sent a shiver down his spine.

Moving his focus, Dion crouched to examine the white carpet. The faint smell of bleach still lingered, evidence of the killer's attempt to cover their tracks. The forensic team had already documented this, but seeing it again reaffirmed the calculated nature of the crime. He walked to the kitchen, noting the set of knives. One was missing, the same style as the knife found at the crime scene and the one discovered in Martin's apartment. It was unlikely both could belong to Lydia's set, suggesting the presence of duplicate sets, a deliberate attempt to mislead the investigation. He scribbled this observation in his notepad, suspecting a red herring.

Dion's gaze wandered to the photographs on the walls, capturing moments from Lydia's glamorous life. Smiling faces at social events, candid shots at luxurious locations, and intimate family gatherings. Each picture painted a story of affluence and success but also hinted at the pressures and enemies that often accompanied such a lifestyle.

Parties, galas, and sunlit vacations adorned the walls, capturing her in moments of joy and opulence. As he studied the images, a pang of nostalgia hit him, pulling him back to his early days as a detective.

***

Back then, Detective Dion was known for his boldness and impulsiveness, traits that both fueled his drive and sometimes clouded his judgment. His early career had been marked by a fierce determination to make a name for himself, a quest for recognition that often overshadowed his careful consideration of all the facts. One case, in particular, had embodied this reckless ambition, his first high-profile investigation involving a wealthy businessman named Andrew Collins. Collins had been accused of embezzlement and fraud, charges that, at the time, seemed straightforward and undeniable. The evidence appeared to be solid: financial records, witness statements, and a seemingly irrefutable paper trail all pointed toward Collins' guilt. Dion, eager to prove his worth and driven by the pressure of high expectations, focused intently on Collins without fully exploring alternative theories or potential defenses.

The trial had proceeded swiftly. The courtroom buzzed with anticipation, the media hungry for the dramatic climax of the case. Collins was convicted, and Dion felt a fleeting sense of triumph as the verdict was delivered. However, this triumph would soon sour into profound regret. It wasn't long before new evidence surfaced, suggesting that Collins had been framed by a rival, a discovery that emerged only after the trial. Despite the growing evidence that could exonerate him, Collins remained behind bars while the appeal process unfolded, a process plagued by delays and bureaucratic red tape.

The true depth of Dion's mistake became glaringly apparent when tragedy struck. Collins' teenage daughter, Emma, fell gravely ill. Despite the mounting evidence of her father's innocence and numerous pleas for compassionate leave, Collins was denied any reprieve from prison. The legal system's inertia, coupled with the harsh reality of his confinement, meant that Collins was helpless as his daughter's condition worsened. Emma passed away, and the news reached Dion with crushing finality.

Sitting in his dimly lit office, surrounded by stacks of case files, Dion received the call that shattered his world. The words "Emma Collins has died" reverberated in his mind, a haunting refrain that underscored the gravity of his misjudgment. In that moment, the weight of his actions settled heavily on his shoulders. He was faced with the devastating realization that a father had lost his daughter while languishing in prison for a crime he did not commit, an innocent life cut short by Dion's hasty and flawed investigation.

This profound failure transformed Dion fundamentally. The case became a ghost that lingered over his career, a constant reminder of the perilous divide between justice and injustice. Where once there had been unbridled confidence, there was now a tempered caution. His decisions became more deliberate, his approach more measured. Every choice was weighed with the knowledge that each misstep carried the potential to irrevocably alter lives. Dion's boldness was tempered with a newfound patience, and his eagerness to solve cases was balanced with a deeper empathy for those affected by his work. The lessons learned from the Collins case remained a somber touchstone, shaping his approach to justice and reminding him of the heavy responsibility borne by those who seek it.

***

As he stood alone in Lydia Harper's penthouse, the weight of his past mistakes bore heavily on Detective Dion. The opulent surroundings, once vibrant with Lydia's life, now seemed to amplify the echoes of his earlier failures. The luxurious decor, once a symbol of success and sophistication, now felt cold and indifferent in the quiet of the evening. The hidden camera embedded behind the false wall, the bleach-stained carpet, and the poignant photographs of Lydia's glamorous life, all these elements were more than just clues; they were fragments of a story that Dion was determined to piece together with precision and care.

This case was not just about solving a murder; it was a chance to atone for his previous missteps, to demonstrate that he had learned from his past and grown as a detective. Lydia deserved justice, a resolution that was both thorough and fair. He was acutely aware that the pressure to solve the case quickly should never come at the expense of accuracy and integrity. Determined to honor her memory and uphold his principles, Dion committed to pursuing every lead with meticulous care.

To Evenings Together

As the day drew to a close, the police team convened in the conference room, a place that had become the war room for the investigation into Lydia Harper's murder. The room was illuminated by harsh, fluorescent lights that flickered overhead, casting a cold, clinical sheen over the gathering. The intense atmosphere was palpable, mirroring the gravity of the case they were grappling with.

Detective Dion Knight, Officer Stevens, and several members of the forensics team were deeply engrossed in their work around the expansive conference table. The surface of the table was a chaotic tapestry of evidence, files, photographs, digital recordings, and a multitude of documents, each contributing to the intricate puzzle they were determined to solve. The once neatly organized stacks of papers and evidence had evolved into an overwhelming array of materials.

On one side of the table, original photographs from the crime scene and detailed profiles of the suspects were spread out. Each image, from close-ups of the crime scene to candid shots of those involved, was meticulously arranged to provide a comprehensive visual representation of the investigation. These photographs were juxtaposed with full statements and follow-up statements from witnesses, suspects, and experts. The latest additions included frames from the hidden camera footage, their grainy quality now a stark reminder of the secrets that Lydia's penthouse had concealed.

The large whiteboard at the front of the room was covered in a sprawling array of notes, diagrams, and sketches. Key points of the investigation were highlighted in different colors, creating a visual map of the case's progression. Arrows and connections between suspects, motives, and timelines were drawn with fervent precision. The whiteboard had become a canvas for the team's collective effort to make sense of the evidence, a tangible representation of their pursuit for clarity amidst the confusion.

Dion stood at the head of the table, his posture rigid and his face a mask of concentration. He reviewed the latest findings with a mix of frustration and determination. The mounting evidence, while crucial, seemed to complicate rather than clarify the path to the truth. His gaze swept over the array of photographs, statements, and forensic reports, each piece a critical element in the complex narrative they were trying to piece together. The weight of the case was heavy on his shoulders, but his resolve remained unshaken. He knew that the answers they sought were hidden within this sea of evidence, waiting to be uncovered with diligence and persistence.

Officer Stevens adjusted his glasses and glanced at the documents scattered across the table. "So, we've confirmed that the footage was tampered with. The gaps and distortions are consistent with deliberate interference, but we haven't identified who had access or motive for the tampering."

Dion nodded, acknowledging the gravity of the situation. "Right. We know the footage was altered to obscure crucial evidence. The question now is who had both the opportunity to do this."

Detective Dion's focus shifted to the large, portable whiteboard tucked away in the corner of the conference room. It had been largely ignored amid the mountain of documents and photographs, but now it seemed to him like the ideal tool for organizing the growing complexity of the case. He wheeled the whiteboard over to the center of the room, positioning it strategically where everyone could easily see. The wheels squeaked slightly, adding a subtle but fitting sound to the intensity of the moment.

He grabbed a marker from the nearby supply tray and began to sketch out the main suspects: Martin Blake, Clara Sullivan, and Gregory Harper. Each name was written in bold letters, with lines extending to various notes and connections, creating a web of potential motives and opportunities.

"Let's break it down," Dion said, his voice carrying a note of resolve as he addressed the room. He pointed to Martin Blake's name on the whiteboard. "Martin Blake is an artist, known for his creative flair and technical skills. It's plausible that he could have manipulated the video footage if he had access to the camera system. We know he has a background in multimedia and digital arts, which might have given him the technical knowledge needed. However, his motive remains somewhat elusive. Martin claims to have been unaware of the affair between Lydia and his colleague, and his alibi, which places him at his art studio during the time of Lydia's death, checks out."

Stevens leaned closer to the whiteboard, his expression thoughtful. "On the other hand, Clara Sullivan has both the financial resources and the business connections that could enable her to hire someone to alter the footage. Her involvement in the heated business dispute with Lydia provides a strong motive, especially considering the public and private fallout from their business dealings. But does she possess the technical skills to manipulate the footage herself? Unlikely. The complexity of the footage tampering suggests a higher level of technical expertise than what Clara would have."

Dion nodded, making a few notes on the whiteboard next to Clara's name. "Clara's financial leverage could indeed allow her to outsource such a task. Given her contentious relationship with Lydia and the potential damage to her business reputation, it's clear she had a motive. However, the technical nature of the footage tampering could also point to someone with artistic or digital manipulation skills, which brings us back to Martin."

He tapped the whiteboard thoughtfully, his brow furrowing as he considered the implications. "We can't completely discount the possibility that Martin's artistic skills might have allowed him to manipulate the footage himself, particularly if he had the opportunity to access the camera system. His alibi and lack of a clear motive are significant, but the evidence points to someone who could both access and alter the footage."

Stevens pulled the laptop from his bag with a practiced motion, setting it on the table with a quiet thud. He opened the lid and began navigating through the various folders and files, his fingers moving swiftly over the keyboard. Dion, feeling a surge of anticipation, pulled up a chair next to him. The soft glow of the laptop screen illuminated their faces as they prepared to delve into the crucial CCTV footage.

The screen flickered to life, and the video feed from the building's security cameras appeared. Stevens tapped a few keys, bringing up a section of footage that showed the area surrounding Lydia Harper's penthouse. The clarity of the video was sharp, and Dion watched intently as the footage played out, seeking any anomalies that might shed light on the case.

"We've identified that someone accessed the camera system," Stevens began, his voice low and steady, "but the records aren't clear about who was responsible. The maintenance logs and security records are all inconclusive. There's no direct evidence linking Martin or Clara to the tampering, which means we might be dealing with an accomplice or possibly a hired professional."

Dion's eyes narrowed as he focused on the screen, his mind racing with the possibilities. The footage showed various angles of the building's hallways and entrances, but there were no clear signs of suspicious activity, at least nothing that jumped out immediately. Dion leaned closer, his gaze scrutinizing every frame as he considered the implications of what they were seeing.

"If Clara did hire someone to manipulate the footage," Dion said thoughtfully, "we need to trace that connection. It's crucial to find out who the hired professional might be. We should also look into Martin's background further, see if he had any associates or contacts who possess the technical skills necessary to tamper with the footage."

Stevens nodded in agreement, his attention still fixed on the laptop screen. "I'll cross-reference Martin's known associates with any technical experts who might fit the profile. At the same time, we should dig deeper into Clara's financial transactions and communications to uncover any clues about a potential hire. There has to be some evidence, however small, that links them to the tampering."

Dion looked around at the team, his expression resolute. "We're at a critical juncture. The tampered footage indicates that someone is trying to hide something, and we need to find out who and why. Our next steps are to investigate both Martin's and Clara's potential connections to the tampering and to verify if anyone else was involved."

It was the end of the day. The investigation has to continue tomorrow. Stevens looks at Detective Dion. "Pub?" He asked.

"Pub."

The day's work finally over, Detective Dion Knight and Officer Stevens sought refuge in a familiar haunt: a local pub just a short walk from the police station. The evening air was cool and crisp, with a gentle breeze rustling the leaves of the trees lining the quiet streets. The sky was painted in shades of twilight, a deep blue gradually giving way to the encroaching darkness. As they walked, the distant hum of the city faded, replaced by the soothing sounds of their footsteps on the cobblestone path. Soon, "The Rusty Anchor" came into view, its old-world charm offering a comforting sight. The cozy haven welcomed them with its dim lighting and rich aroma of aged wood mingled with the faint scent of spilt ale. Overhead, tarnished brass lamps cast a warm, mellow glow, bathing the room in a soft, amber hue.

The murmurs of quiet conversations filled the space, mingling with the gentle strains of country music that drifted from a jukebox in the corner. The floorboards creaked underfoot as patrons shifted in their seats, and the occasional clink of glassware punctuated the otherwise subdued ambiance. The walls were adorned with vintage nautical memorabilia, adding a touch of character to the dimly lit interior.

Dion and Stevens approached the bar, where a grizzled bartender with a knowing smile stood ready to serve. The bartender, a man in his late fifties with a thick, gray beard and eyes that seemed to have witnessed a lifetime of stories, greeted them with a nod. His hands were steady and experienced, moving with the practiced ease of someone who had spent decades behind the bar. The walls behind him were lined with an eclectic collection of liquor bottles, each reflecting the soft, amber glow of the pub's lighting. The well-worn bar counter, polished to a sheen by countless hands over the years, added to the pub's inviting atmosphere.

Dion ordered a pint of stout, the dark beer promising a hearty flavor to match the end of a long day. His demeanor was serious and contemplative, reflecting the weight of the cases he handled and the dedication he brought to his work. The stout, with its rich and robust taste, suited his character perfectly, no-nonsense and substantial.

Stevens, however, opted for something lighter, a pink gin with lemonade and half a strawberry for garnish. His choice mirrored his lighter, more effervescent personality. As the bartender deftly prepared the drink, Stevens chatted amiably, his voice carrying a hint of laughter that seemed to brighten the dim pub. His drink was a splash of color against the rustic background, much like his personality added a lively distinction to Dion's more somber presence.

As they settled into their seats, Stevens took a sip of his gin and lemonade and cast a sideways glance at Dion. The detective's face was etched with the weariness of the case, but the familiarity of the pub seemed to offer a moment of respite.

"Hey, Dion," Stevens began casually, breaking the comfortable silence that had settled between them. "You've been working this job for a long time. Ever think about settling down, maybe getting married?"

Dion raised an eyebrow, his gaze fixed on the frothy head of his stout. He took a slow sip before replying. "Marriage, huh? I've had my share of chances. But honestly, it's a complicated business. Sometimes, it feels like marriage just drives people to do foolish things."

Stevens looked curious but listened attentively. "Foolish things? Like what do you mean?"

Dion leaned back in his chair, his expression thoughtful. "People often make decisions based on emotion rather than logic. In a relationship, emotions can cloud judgment and lead to actions that don't always make sense. I've seen it firsthand, people compromising their principles, making rash decisions, or even resorting to deceit to keep their relationships intact."

Stevens nodded slowly, processing Dion's words. "I suppose that makes sense. It's easy to get swept up in the moment and make decisions that aren't always rational. But isn't there something to be said for having someone to share your life with, even if it's complicated?"

Dion offered a small, wistful smile. "There's definitely value in companionship, but it's a balance. Sometimes the risk of losing yourself in someone else's problems outweighs the benefits. I guess I've learned to keep my distance, focus on the job, and let the rest fall where it may."

Stevens took a thoughtful sip of his gin and lemonade, reflecting on Dion's perspective. "I get that. It's hard to find the right balance between personal life and professional duties. But don't you ever think about what you're missing out on?"

Dion shrugged lightly, a hint of a smile playing at the corners of his lips. "Maybe. But right now, my focus is on the case. There's plenty to unravel and solve, and I'm not sure I'd have the same drive if I were distracted by other things."

Stevens drained the last of his gin and rose to get another round. "Same again?" he asked. Dion nodded absently, lost in thought. As Stevens weaved through the crowd, Dion's mind wandered back to the case, the images of the penthouse mingling with the ghosts of his past mistakes. "Emma Collins has died." The words echoed in his mind, a haunting refrain that never fully left him. He could see her father's grief-stricken face, feel the weight of his own culpability in every decision he'd made since.

His reverie was interrupted by the return of Stevens, a fresh beverage in each hand, his face glowing with the warmth of alcohol and camaraderie. "Here you go," Stevens said, sliding a drink towards Dion and sitting down heavily in his chair.

Dion took a sip, the bitter taste of a dark stout grounding him back to the present. "Stevens," he began, his voice thoughtful, "who do you think did it?"

Without missing a beat, Stevens replied, "It's probably Martin. He's got the motive, and that knife in his apartment... it's too suspicious to ignore."

Dion leaned back, his eyes narrowing slightly. "Be careful, Stevens. Remember, we can't afford to jump to conclusions. We've been burned by that before." He paused, taking another sip of his drink, his gaze distant. "Every piece of evidence should be considered, and every lead followed. We owe it to Lydia to get this right, and we owe it to ourselves not to repeat past mistakes."

Stevens nodded, his enthusiasm slightly dimmed but his respect for Dion evident. "I get it, boss. But don't you think sometimes your gut feeling can lead you to the truth?"

"Sometimes," Dion conceded, "but the gut can also be swayed by biases and emotions. We need the facts, Stevens. Only the facts."

Stevens took a deep gulp of his gin, contemplating Dion's words. "Alright, then. We'll keep digging, no matter how long it takes."

Their conversation drifted into lighter topics, the weight of the day's investigation temporarily lifted by the casual atmosphere of the pub. The country music played softly in the background, creating a comforting soundtrack to their evening of camaraderie. The song shifted, and Stevens' face lit up as his favorite tune began to play.

"Hey, Dion, you know this one?" Stevens asked, grinning widely as he started to dance in his seat. He moved his shoulders to the beat, tapping his foot on the wooden floor. "Come on, loosen up a bit!"

Dion, ever the serious detective, rolled his eyes but couldn't help the small smile tugging at the corners of his mouth. "You know I'm not much of a dancer, Stevens."

"Oh, come on, just one move!" Stevens laughed, his joy infectious. He clapped his hands and swayed, urging Dion to join in.

With a resigned sigh, Dion put down his pint and stood up. He threw a quick glance around the pub, making sure no one was watching too closely. Then, with a hint of mischief in his eyes, he executed a brief, awkward dance move, shuffling his feet and swinging his hips for a second. Stevens erupted into laughter, clapping his hands in delight.

"There you go! See, that wasn't so hard, was it?" Stevens beamed, still dancing in his seat.

Dion shook his head, but his smile lingered. "Alright, alright, you got your dance. Now let's get back to the drinks."

They both took a sip, the tension of the day melting away in the warm, dimly lit embrace of the pub. Stevens continued to hum along with the song, his good mood lifting Dion's spirits. For a brief moment, the relentless pursuit of justice was put on hold, replaced by a simple, shared joy.

The bartender, noticing their moment of respite, approached with a knowing smile. "Another round, gentlemen?" he offered, his voice a gravelly murmur.

Dion nodded. "Sure, why not? It's been one hell of a day."

As the bartender poured their drinks, Dion glanced around the pub. The familiar faces of regulars, the comforting hum of conversation, and the soft clinking of glasses created a sense of belonging that contrasted sharply with the day's chaos. Here, in the midst of the Rusty Anchor's cozy atmosphere, he found a brief sanctuary.

Stevens clinked his glass against Dion's. "To finding the truth."

Under Pressure

The morning sun streamed through the narrow windows of the police station, casting a pale light over the bustling workspace. Officer Stevens was already at his desk, his demeanor energetic and bright as he meticulously organized files and prepared for the day ahead. His optimism was a striking difference to the weary figure that ambled through the door shortly afterward. Detective Dion Knight entered the station, his steps heavy and deliberate. The previous night's reprieve at the pub had been fleeting, and the weight of the ongoing investigation quickly settled back onto his shoulders.

Detective Dion Knight shuffled into the office, his movements sluggish and his face etched with the unmistakable signs of a hangover. Dark circles underlined his eyes, and he moved with a deliberate caution, each step a testament to the night's indulgences. He winced as the overhead lights seemed to amplify his discomfort, but he pushed through, driven by the pressing demands of the case.

Stevens looked up from his desk, a broad smile spreading across his face. "Morning, Dion! How's the head this morning?"

Dion grunted in response, rubbing his temples. "Morning, Stevens. Let's just say I'm feeling the effects of last night."

Stevens chuckled, clearly in high spirits. "Yeah, we had a good time at the pub. It was nice getting to know you a bit better. You don't usually let your guard down like that."

Dion grunted again, not entirely interested in reliving the previous evening's conversations. "Sure, Stevens. I appreciate the bonding, but right now, we've got a case to solve."

Stevens nodded, his enthusiasm undiminished. "Right, right. We need to follow up on the new evidence. The tampering with the secret camera might give us new insights into the case."

Dion took a seat at his desk, letting out a sigh as he opened his laptop. "Exactly. We need to bring Clara Sullivan and Martin Blake in for questioning again. We have to see how they react to the news about the tampered footage."

Stevens pulled up the case file on his computer, his fingers flying over the keyboard. "We should prepare questions that address their possible involvement with the tampering. It'll be crucial to see if either of them reacts defensively or shows signs of guilt."

Dion nodded, his focus sharpening despite his lingering hangover. "We need to get their responses and see if there are inconsistencies in their stories. The tampered footage could be the key to unraveling this whole mess."

Stevens agreed, pulling out the evidence files related to Clara and Martin. "I'll make sure we're ready with the right questions. We need to catch them off guard and see if they slip up."

Before they could set their plan into motion, a summons from the Chief Constable interrupted their preparations. The two detectives were called into the Chief Constable's office, a space that was as immaculate as it was dimly lit. The room was decorated with high-backed leather chairs and polished mahogany furniture, a sharp divergence from the chaotic energy of the police station outside.

Chief Constable Harris was seated behind his desk, his face partially obscured by a cloud of vapor. He was puffing on a sleek, new strawberry-flavored vape pen, though he seemed to be struggling with the unfamiliar device. His eyes squinted as he exhaled, coughing slightly as he tried to clear the sweet, fruity vapor from his throat.

"Dion, Stevens," Harris said with a raspy voice, his attempts to manage the vape still evident. "Glad you could make it. Come in, have a seat."

Dion and Stevens entered, taking their places opposite the Chief Constable. Dion couldn't help but notice the strong, artificial scent of strawberries that lingered in the air, a jarring contrast to the otherwise serious atmosphere of the office.

Harris, still clearing his throat, glanced at them with a look of growing impatience. "This newfangled vape doesn't quite hit the spot. Smoking was such an easier time, but I digress."

He leaned forward, his expression hardening as he focused on the matter at hand. "The media attention on this case is escalating rapidly. We're facing mounting pressure from every direction. The public is demanding answers, and I need this case solved quickly."

Dion met Harris's gaze, the weight of the Chief Constable's words pressing down on him. "We're on it, sir. We've identified that the secret camera footage was tampered with, and we plan to re-interview Clara Sullivan and Martin Blake to assess their reactions and see if they reveal anything new."

Harris nodded curtly, his irritation barely concealed. "Good. We need results, and we need them fast. This case is turning into a media circus, and I won't have our department's reputation dragged through the mud."

Stevens, trying to maintain a positive outlook despite the Chief Constable's stern demeanor, chimed in. "We're working diligently on it, Chief. We're confident that addressing the tampered footage with Clara and Martin will yield useful information."

Harris gave a terse nod, clearly eager to move past the discussion of the vape and onto the urgency of the case. "Make it happen. The sooner we have answers, the better. The public's patience is wearing thin, and we need to show them that justice is being served."

With that, Harris waved them off, returning to his attempts with the vape pen. Dion and Stevens exchanged a glance as they exited the office, the weight of the Chief Constable's urgency settling heavily upon them.

Despite the groggy haze that lingered over Dion, the weight of the investigation pressed heavily on him. Each piece of evidence, each suspect's reaction, was a potential step toward solving Lydia Harper's murder.

Stevens continued to buzz with energy, making final adjustments to the interview questions and reviewing the case files. Dion, though still feeling the aftereffects of the previous night, focused on piecing together the investigation's intricacies. The dynamic between the two was a blend of energy and exhaustion, a balance of enthusiasm and resolve.

The interview room was a bare, functional space: a rectangular table surrounded by hard, uncomfortable chairs, with a one-way mirror on one wall. The room was softly lit, creating an interplay of light and shadow that seemed to amplify the sense of unease. Dion took his place at one end of the table, preparing for another round of questioning. Martin Blake was already seated on the opposite side, his posture relaxed but his eyes betraying a hint of nervousness.

Martin looked up as Dion entered, offering a tight-lipped smile that did little to mask his anxiety. "Good to see you again, Detective."

Dion took a seat and regarded Martin with a measured gaze. "Martin, we need to talk about the hidden camera found at Lydia Harper's penthouse. We've discovered that the footage from that camera was tampered with. I need to know if you have any knowledge of this."

Martin's expression remained calm, though his eyes flickered with a trace of concern. "I've already told you, Detective, I don't know anything about a hidden camera. I had no idea there was one in Lydia's apartment."

Dion leaned forward, his tone becoming more insistent. "The footage was altered, Martin. This indicates someone had access to the camera system and deliberately manipulated the evidence. Do you have any idea who might have done this? Or perhaps, did you notice anything suspicious around the time of Lydia's death?"

Martin shook his head slowly, his demeanor unruffled. "No, Detective. I didn't know about the camera, and I certainly didn't tamper with any footage. I was shocked to learn about Lydia's death, and I've cooperated with the investigation as much as I can."

Dion narrowed his eyes, scrutinizing Martin's calm facade. "You're saying you had no knowledge of the camera or the tampering? We've reviewed the evidence and it seems clear that someone with access and technical know-how was involved. The footage was deliberately altered to obscure critical moments."

Martin's voice remained steady, though a subtle tension was evident in his shoulders. "I'm telling you the truth. I didn't have anything to do with it. If you have evidence that suggests otherwise, I'd like to see it. But I assure you, I had no involvement with the camera or the footage."

Dion's patience was wearing thin, but he maintained his composure. "Alright, Martin. For now, we'll note your statement. We haven't been able to confirm your alibi yet either…"

As Martin left the interview room, Dion remained seated, deep in thought. Martin's responses were consistent with his previous statements, but the calmness and assurance in his demeanor were unsettling. If Martin were involved in tampering with the footage, he was concealing it well.

The minutes ticked by as Detective Dion Knight waited in the dimly lit interview room, the stillness of the space amplifying his growing anticipation. He reviewed his notes and mentally prepared his strategy for the upcoming interrogation. Clara Sullivan was due to arrive any moment, and Dion was ready to challenge her on the newly discovered tampering with the hidden camera footage.

The door to the interview room swung open, and Clara Sullivan stepped inside. Her entrance was as controlled and poised as ever; she walked with an air of deliberate calmness, her designer suit impeccably tailored and her expression meticulously composed. She took her seat at the table with a practiced grace, her posture rigid as if bracing for the upcoming questioning.

"Detective Knight," Clara greeted with a clipped tone, her voice betraying no sign of the unease that Dion suspected lay beneath the surface.

"Ms. Sullivan," Dion responded, his gaze steady as he took his seat across from her. "Thank you for coming in. I'd like to revisit our discussion in light of new developments. We've discovered that the footage from the hidden camera in Lydia Harper's penthouse was tampered with."

Clara's eyes narrowed slightly, though her face remained a mask of professionalism. "I see. And how does this concern me, Detective?"

Dion leaned forward, studying Clara's reaction closely. "We need to know if you have any information regarding this tampering. The alterations to the footage suggest that someone with technical expertise and access was involved. You're aware that the camera was hidden in a location that only someone with intimate knowledge of the apartment would know about."

Clara's gaze flickered, but she quickly regained her composure. "I have no knowledge of any hidden camera or tampering with footage. My involvement in Lydia's affairs was strictly professional. I don't see how this is related to me."

Dion's voice was measured, though a hint of insistence crept in. "The footage being doctored means crucial evidence was concealed. We're trying to understand who had the means and motive to manipulate it. Your financial disputes with Lydia, the public fallout, these are relevant details. Was there anyone in your circle who might have had the skills or the reason to interfere with the investigation?"

Clara's fingers tightened around the edge of the table, her knuckles turning white. "I've already explained that I had no personal stake in Lydia's death beyond our business disagreements. My team and I had no reason to interfere with any investigation. If someone is manipulating evidence, it's not something I condone or have any involvement in."

Dion noticed the subtle shift in Clara's demeanor. Her previously cool, distant façade now showed traces of strain, particularly in the way her jaw tightened and her eyes darted slightly. "Ms. Sullivan, I must emphasize that tampering with evidence is a serious matter. If you're withholding information or if there's something you're not telling us, it's in your best interest to be forthcoming. This case is being scrutinized heavily, and your cooperation could make a difference."

Clara's breath hitched imperceptibly, and she shifted uncomfortably in her chair. Her calm mask was slipping, revealing the faintest tremor of anxiety. "Detective, I assure you, I am as cooperative as possible. I don't have any more information than what I've already provided. If someone else is involved, it's beyond my knowledge."

Dion studied her intently, noting every nuance of her reaction. The anxiety she displayed, though subtle, was telling. There was something in her response that did not entirely align with her earlier statements, suggesting she might be concealing something or at least holding back key details.

As the interview came to a close, Dion leaned back. Clara stood and adjusted her suit, her composure somewhat restored but her eyes betraying a flicker of unease. Clara exited the room, Dion remained seated, deep in thought. Clara's reactions had provided valuable insight, though the full extent of her involvement remained unclear. The subtle signs of anxiety she displayed could indicate more than just a professional concern.

As the interview with Clara Sullivan concluded, Detective Dion Knight exited the interview room and made his way back to his desk. Officer Stevens was already there, having spent the intervening time verifying the details of Martin Blake's alibi. The office buzzed with activity as detectives and officers moved with purpose, their conversations a low murmur in the background.

Dion approached Stevens, who had been diligently reviewing the CCTV footage from the docks. As Dion approached, Stevens looked up with a determined expression. "Martin's alibi checks out," Stevens announced. "The CCTV footage shows his car arriving at the art studio by the docks about ten minutes before Lydia was killed, and it didn't move until the following morning. A security guard from the building across the street confirmed seeing the car parked there all night."

Dion sat down at his desk, running a hand through his hair. "That's consistent with what he said during the interview. So it seems Martin is off the hook for this one."

Stevens nodded, glancing at the documents on his desk. "Yeah, and the security footage from the hotel confirms his presence. He was signed in at the event and didn't leave until after midnight. That matches up with the timeline we have for Lydia's murder."

As the two detectives continued their discussion, the office's usual hum of activity became a backdrop to their focused conversation. The investigation into Lydia Harper's murder had taken several turns, and with Martin Blake's alibi confirmed, the spotlight shifted to Clara Sullivan. The challenge now was to substantiate Clara's involvement with concrete evidence. Alternatively, they considered the possibility that someone else might have been tasked with the crime.

The Blackmail Plot

The clock ticked past midnight as Detective Dion Knight and Officer Stevens remained huddled over their desks in the dimly lit police station. The normally bustling precinct was eerily quiet, the hum of fluorescent lights casting a sterile glow over the deserted space. The clatter of keyboards and the rustle of papers were the only sounds breaking the silence, punctuated occasionally by the soft echo of footsteps from a solitary cleaner making her rounds. The weight of their task hung heavy in the air, as they meticulously combed through the evidence, determined to find the crucial piece that would unravel the case.

The cleaner moved methodically down the corridor, her mop trailing behind her in rhythmic sweeps. Her presence was a faint but reassuring reminder of the station's ongoing pulse, even as the rest of the building lay dormant. She passed by the open door of the detectives' office, the faint clinking of her cleaning supplies a soft backdrop to the intense concentration of Dion and Stevens.

Dion and Stevens sat surrounded by a labyrinth of paperwork and digital files, their faces illuminated by the cold light of their computer screens. The weight of the investigation hung heavily in the air, as if the very walls of the station were saturated with the tension of their relentless pursuit. Dion's sharp eyes darted across the documents, occasionally glancing at the clock and then back at the evidence, his brow furrowed in deep thought.

Stevens, seated beside him, flipped through a stack of printouts with a focused intensity. "We've been at this for hours," he said, his voice barely more than a whisper in the quiet room. "There has to be something we've missed."

Dion nodded, his gaze fixed on a series of emails on his screen. "We need to dig deeper. The more we uncover, the clearer the picture becomes. Lydia's blackmail scheme could be the key to understanding why someone might have felt cornered enough to kill her."

The station's emptiness seemed to amplify their sense of isolation, the long hours of work stretching endlessly before them. Dion's fingers tapped rhythmically on the keyboard as he scrolled through Lydia Harper's financial records, while Stevens cross-referenced the data with other investigative reports.

The night wore on, each minute marked by the steady, methodical pace of their work. The murky light and the faint, echoing footsteps of the cleaner created an almost surreal backdrop for their relentless quest for answers. The case was evolving, and every new detail brought them a step closer to the truth. The atmosphere in the station felt like the calm before a storm, charged with anticipation and the promise of breakthroughs that would soon come to light.

As the cleaner moved down the hallway, her presence a distant hum in the background, Dion and Stevens remained engrossed in their task, driven by the urgent need to piece together the last fragments of a complex puzzle.

"Got something interesting here," Stevens said, dropping a thick manila folder on Dion's desk with a soft thud. His eyes sparkled with a mix of excitement and anticipation as he took a seat next to Dion.

Dion, already feeling the weight of the day's investigation pressing down on him, looked up with renewed interest. "What did you find?" he asked, his voice steady but laced with curiosity.

Stevens opened the folder to reveal a collection of printed emails and handwritten letters, each meticulously organized and clearly marked. He laid the documents out on the desk, the scent of fresh ink mingling with the stale air of the office. "I've been digging through Lydia's emails, and I think we've hit something significant," Stevens said, his tone almost reverent. "These emails detail a series of demands Lydia made to Clara Sullivan."

Dion leaned forward, his eyes narrowing as he began to sift through the papers. The first email was dated several months prior, the subject line bluntly stating, *'Final Warning'*. The message was terse, Lydia's tone sharp and uncompromising.

***

Clara,

This is your final notice. If I do not receive the payment of $500,000 by the end of the week, I will go public with the information I have. You know what I mean. This isn't a game. The clock is ticking.

Lydia.

***

Dion's eyebrows furrowed as he scanned the subsequent emails, his mind racing to process the gravity of what he was uncovering. The next few messages revealed a series of increasingly desperate pleas from Clara, each one marked by a growing sense of urgency and fear. Clara's words were fraught with anxiety, her attempts to negotiate a lower sum of money evident in every line. Her responses were a mix of apologies, promises of future payment, and emotional appeals, trying to buy herself more time.

Lydia's replies, however, were stark and unyielding. Her tone was a cold, unrelenting demand for payment, showing no sign of mercy or willingness to negotiate. The threats in Lydia's messages were unmistakable, leaving no room for misinterpretation. It was clear Lydia had held a firm and unforgiving stance, prepared to expose Clara's secrets if her demands were not met.

As Dion absorbed the content of the emails, he felt a surge of realization. This new evidence provided a crucial piece of the puzzle, revealing the intense pressure and desperation Clara had been under. His brow furrowed deeper as he considered the implications. The blackmail scheme had not only created a volatile environment but had likely driven Clara to a breaking point, potentially motivating her to resort to extreme measures.

A final message caught Dion's eyes:

***

Clara,

You've had ample time. I'm not interested in haggling. Either you come up with the full amount, or I expose everything.

***

The level of detail in the emails was damning. Lydia had clearly been leveraging some form of compromising information about Clara, and the stakes were high. Dion's mind raced as he connected the dots. Blackmail was a powerful motive, Clara's potential financial ruin or personal disgrace could have pushed her to extreme measures, especially if Lydia's demands had become unbearable.

Stevens glanced at Dion, his excitement palpable. "This could be huge.

Clara had a clear motive to want Lydia out of the way. If this information got out, it would have devastated her career and possibly her entire life. This blackmail scheme could have driven her to drastic actions."

Dion nodded, his mind already piecing together the implications. "It fits with the timeline. If Lydia was pressuring Clara and Clara felt cornered, she might have sought to eliminate her threat. We need to dig deeper into Clara's finances and communications to confirm if she was involved in hiring someone to manipulate the footage or, worse, to commit the murder."

Stevens's excitement grew.

"This," Dion said, tapping a particularly damning email, "could be the motive we've been missing. If Clara was being blackmailed, she'd have a powerful reason to silence Lydia. This also explains the tension we observed in Clara's responses during her interview."

Stevens nodded, his expression thoughtful. "And this adds a new layer to the case. If Clara was under pressure, it's possible she might have seen no other way out than to take drastic measures."

Dion's mind considers all angles. The blackmail scheme painted a picture of desperation and betrayal. But how did this connect with the tampered footage?

"Clara's alibi checks out, but Lydia's failure to appear at the business dinner suggests she was already in trouble," Dion mused. "If Clara was at the dinner and Lydia was supposed to be there but wasn't, we need to reconstruct what happened during that time. The blackmail plot adds a new dimension to the motive, but we still need to determine how it fits with the evidence we have."

Stevens leaned back, considering the next steps. "We should also think about the possibility of someone else being involved. If Clara was desperate enough to consider silencing Lydia, she might have turned to someone else for help. Or maybe someone discovered the scheme and acted on their own."

As the early hours of the morning approached, Detective Dion Knight and Officer Stevens meticulously compiled their findings related to Lydia Harper's blackmail scheme. They reviewed each document, cross-referenced the emails with Lydia's financial records, and prepared a comprehensive summary of their new lead.

Dion sat back in his chair, staring at the ceiling as he mulled over the evidence. A troubling thought raced through his mind: Was the evidence compelling enough, or could it be a meticulously laid trap? The complexity of the case left him questioning every detail, wary of the possibility that they were being led astray by a cunning adversary. He knew they had to tread carefully, ensuring that their pursuit of justice remained unwavering and precise.

As the question gnawed at him, Dion's mind drifted back to a pivotal moment from his childhood. He was eight years old, and his father, Thomas Knight, had just returned home with a triumphant gleam in his eye. The investigative journalist, renowned for his tenacity and unerring sense of justice; Dion's hero and mentor. That night, he had made a breakthrough in a case that had haunted him for months.

***

Dion vividly remembered sitting at the kitchen table, his small hands clutching a glass of milk as he watched his father spread out a series of documents and photographs across the worn wooden surface. The kitchen, with its faded yellow wallpaper and scuffed linoleum floor, was bathed in the warm, flickering light of a single overhead bulb. The air was thick with the comforting aroma of his mother's cooking, mingling with the faint scent of old paper and ink from the documents.

Thomas's face was etched with lines of fatigue, dark circles under his eyes betraying the countless sleepless nights he had endured. Despite this, his eyes shone with excitement and determination. He explained to Dion, in simple terms, how he had uncovered a corruption scandal involving a prominent city official. Thomas had meticulously pieced together the evidence, following a trail of deceit and manipulation that had led him to the truth.

The table was a chaotic array of papers, photographs, and handwritten notes, each piece a crucial part of the puzzle. Dion's gaze darted from one document to another, his young mind trying to make sense of the intricate web his father had unraveled. There were grainy black-and-white photos of clandestine meetings, bank statements showing suspicious transactions, and transcripts of whispered conversations caught on tape.

Thomas pointed out key pieces of evidence, his voice animated as he described the painstaking work that had gone into gathering and connecting each piece. "See this, Dion? This is a record of a payment made to a shell company. And here, this photo shows the official meeting with the company's supposed owner. It's all connected, you just have to see the patterns."

Dion was fascinated, his eyes wide with awe and curiosity. He could feel the excitement in his father's voice, the thrill of uncovering a hidden truth. But what struck him most that night wasn't the breakthrough itself, but the lesson his father imparted in the aftermath.

Thomas leaned back in his chair, the weight of the moment settling over them both. "Always be thorough, son," Thomas had said, his voice steady but imbued with a seriousness that Dion rarely heard. "The truth is often buried beneath layers of deception. And sometimes, what appears to be a breakthrough might just be another trap. You must be certain before you act, because the cost of a mistake can be high."

He paused, his expression softening as he looked at Dion. "When you rush, you miss things. Important things. Details that could change everything. Patience and diligence are your best tools in uncovering the truth. Remember that, Dion."

***

Snapping back to the present, Dion felt the familiar weight of that lesson pressing upon him. The evidence against Clara was substantial, but was it too perfect? Could it have been planted to mislead them? He glanced at Stevens, who was still engrossed in the documents, his brow furrowed in concentration.

"We need to be absolutely sure about this," Dion said, his voice cutting through the quiet. "Let's go over everything again. We can't afford to be wrong."

Stevens glanced at the clock and then at Dion, his fatigue evident despite the focus in his eyes. "I'll send this over to the tech team for them to review first thing tomorrow. They'll need to analyze how this blackmail plot fits with the rest of the evidence."

Dion nodded, his expression reflecting the exhaustion of the long night. "Good idea. The sooner we get this to them, the sooner we'll have a clearer picture of what really happened. We need to find out how this fits into the timeline and if it influenced anyone's actions that night."

With their tasks completed, the two detectives began to tidy up their workspace. The piles of documents and open files were gathered, and the last of the evidence was neatly organized. The once-bustling office now felt even quieter, the distant sound of the cleaner's mop the only reminder of life beyond the walls of the precinct.

As they prepared to leave, Stevens broke the silence, a casual tone in his voice despite the late hour. "You know, Dion, it's interesting. We've seen all sorts of intense situations in the station. But I wonder, if things ever got so heated professionally, like, really intense, would it ever push someone to do something as drastic as murder?"

Dion paused, his hand resting on the door handle. He looked over at Stevens, his face inscrutable. The question seemed to linger in the air, a probing thought about the nature of human desperation and moral boundaries.

After a moment of silence, Dion chose not to answer. Instead, he offered a small nod and a weary smile. "Let's just say, we deal with the evidence and let it guide us. Sometimes, the motives are clearer once all the pieces are in place."

Stevens appeared to accept the non-answer with a thoughtful nod, though the question seemed to linger in his mind. Both men knew that the pressure and emotional strain of their work could sometimes push people to the brink, but the specifics of such extremes were often left unspoken.

Officer Stevens sighed and checked his watch - 1:30am. "I better head home," he said, rubbing his tired eyes. "My wife's not going to be thrilled with me coming in this late again." Dion nodded in agreement, however not quite understanding the strain long hours can put on personal lives.

With their duties for the night concluded, the two detectives gathered their belongings and exited the station, leaving the quiet office behind. The cleaner, still methodically working her way through the building, continued her routine, her presence a soft, persistent reminder of the passage of time.

As Dion and Stevens headed out into the cool night air, the city lights flickering against the darkness, they each reflected on the challenges of their work and the intricacies of the case. After bidding Stevens goodnight, Dion made his way to his own apartment. The city streets, now illuminated by the moon and the occasional streetlamp, were quieter than usual, with only the occasional car passing by and the distant hum of midnight traffic. Dion's apartment building loomed ahead, a modern structure that juxtaposed sharply with the historic charm of the surrounding city. The sleek lines and glass facade of the building were a reminder of the constant push and pull between the past and the present, mirroring the intricacies of the case that occupied his thoughts.

Entering the building, Dion took the elevator to the 4th floor, where his apartment was situated. The hallway was dimly lit, casting long shadows on the walls. He unlocked his door with a practiced hand and stepped inside, immediately feeling the comforting embrace of familiarity.

His apartment was modest but well-kept, reflecting his preference for simplicity, after all Dion is hardly here. The living room, though small, was inviting. It featured a worn leather sofa that had seen better days, a wooden coffee table cluttered with magazines, and a few framed photographs of past cases and personal moments. A soft light from a nearby lamp cast a warm glow across the room, illuminating the spartan décor and a bookshelf lined with an eclectic mix of novels and case files.

Dion moved quietly, his steps muffled by the plush rug on the floor. He set down his keys and coat on a nearby rack, the fatigue of the day pressing heavily on his shoulders. The quiet of his apartment was welcoming. He moved to the kitchen, where he made himself a quick, velvet hot chocolate to help wind down.

Dion's small kitchen was a blend of practicality and understated charm, reflecting his no-nonsense approach to life. It was a compact space, efficiently designed to make the most of every inch. The walls were painted a soft, neutral beige, providing a warm backdrop to the functional yet cozy setting.

To the right of the entrance, a modest stove and oven sat snugly against the wall, its surface in pristine condition; like it had never been used. A set of simple wooden cabinets, their doors painted in a matching shade of beige.

The sink, placed under a small window, offered a view of the city below. It was a deep, stainless-steel basin, surrounded by a modest counter space covered with neatly organized utensils and a small dish rack.

To the left, a compact coffee maker, well-used and slightly chipped, occupied a corner of the counter. Next to it, a few neatly stacked coffee mugs awaited their daily ritual.

A small wooden table, barely big enough for two, was set against the opposite wall. It was adorned with a simple cloth placemat and a small vase holding a solitary, wilted flower, an endearing touch that added a hint of warmth to the room. A single, wooden chair, its surface polished but showing signs of age, completed the ensemble.

On the far wall, a narrow shelf displayed a modest collection of cookbooks and a few decorative items, including a small potted plant that struggled to thrive in the dim light. The kitchen's compactness did not hinder its functionality; it was a space where Dion could prepare meals with ease, a small sanctuary from the more chaotic aspects of his life.

As he sat down at his kitchen table, Dion reflected on the day's events, the blackmail plot bringing a new layer of complexity to the case. The challenge ahead felt daunting, but he was determined to see it through. With a heavy sigh, he took a sip of his hot chocolate, savoring the warmth and the brief respite from the relentless pace of the investigation. The silence of his apartment offered a moment of calm; Dion was alone. It was time to get some sleep.

The Night of the Murder

The first light of dawn barely pierced the blinds of the police station as Detective Dion Knight walked back in, still shaking off the remnants of the previous night's exhaustion. Officer Stevens was already there, looking surprisingly refreshed. He was hunched over a computer, his face illuminated by the screen's glow.

"Morning, Stevens," Dion greeted, stifling a yawn. "Anything new?"

Stevens looked up, his eyes bright with determination. "Morning, Dion. I've got something. I managed to confirm Clara's alibi. I contacted several attendees of that business dinner, and they all verified her presence there from start to finish. She couldn't have left unnoticed."

Dion nodded, feeling a mix of relief and frustration. "That clears her from being physically present at the scene. But it doesn't rule out her involvement entirely. Let's take this to the boardroom and go over everything again."

The boardroom presented an obvious difference from the dark and cluttered offices they had been working in. As they walked through the door, they were met with an environment that was both imposing and meticulously organized. A large, polished wooden table dominated the center of the room, its surface gleaming under the harsh fluorescent lights. The table was an intricate mosaic of documents, photographs, and items from the crime scene, each piece carefully placed to reconstruct the night of Lydia Harper's murder. The rich wood of the table contrasted vividly with the sterile white walls, which were adorned with whiteboards covered in detailed diagrams, timelines, and photographs of key evidence.

The walls were lined with a mix of legal documents and forensic reports, each taped directly to the walls. Diagrams sketched in neat, precise lines outlined the sequence of events, while timelines traced the crucial moments leading up to and following Lydia's death. On one whiteboard, a large map of the penthouse was marked with colored markers, showing the locations of key evidence and suspect movements.

As Dion and Stevens entered, closing the door behind them, the room was enveloped in an almost reverent silence. The air was filled with a sense of purpose and intensity, broken only by the rustle of paper as they began to sort through the evidence once more. Dion moved with a deliberate pace, carefully laying out the new documents and cross-referencing them with the existing ones. The sound of his fingers tapping against the polished surface of the table seemed to punctuate the gravity of their task.

Stevens joined him, pulling up a chair and setting down a stack of reports. He began organizing the documents into neat piles, grouping them by relevance and chronology. Each photograph and piece of evidence was scrutinized with renewed focus, as they worked to weave together the complex narrative that had unfolded. The atmosphere was charged with a palpable sense of determination as they revisited the details of Lydia Harper's murder, knowing that their next steps could be critical in unraveling the case.

Dion took a moment to survey the table, letting his eyes trace the narrative they had built. There were photographs of Lydia Harper, both in life and in death. Her smiling face contrasted sharply with the grisly crime scene images. Nearby, printouts of email exchanges between Lydia and Clara highlighted the blackmail scheme, their contents revealing a desperate and escalating conflict.

In the center of the table lay a detailed map of the penthouse, annotated with notes on the positions of key evidence. The bloody knife, its handle wiped clean of prints save for Martin's, was depicted prominently. Beside it were forensic reports, detailing the absence of definitive DNA evidence and the puzzling state of the hidden camera footage.

Stevens placed a fresh stack of statements from witnesses at the business dinner next to Clara's file. "Clara was there the entire evening. This is ironclad."

Dion sighed, running a hand through his hair. "That means all our suspects have alibis. Gregory at his event, Martin with witnesses, and now Clara. We're back to square one."

He leaned over the table, focusing on the map of the penthouse. "We need to reconstruct the timeline precisely. Lydia was supposed to attend that dinner, but she never showed. We know someone argued with her before she left her apartment. The hidden camera footage holds the key, but until we can restore the missing moments, we're guessing in the dark."

Stevens nodded, looking over the intricate web of evidence. "The argument must have been about blackmail. If we can identify who had the most to lose, we might narrow down our search. But with all their alibis holding up, it feels like someone hired a professional."

Dion straightened, determination hardening his features. "We need to push the tech team harder on restoring that footage. The argument caught on camera might tell us who orchestrated this. And we need to consider financial records, phone calls, anything that could hint at someone hiring a killer."

They continued to pore over the evidence, the weight of their task pressing down on them. Each photograph, document, and map detail told part of the story, but the crucial pieces remained just out of reach. The boardroom felt like a microcosm of their investigation, a labyrinth of clues waiting for the right key to unlock the truth.

Detective Dion Knight and Officer Stevens settled deeper into their seats, the gravity of the case pulling them into a focused silence. Dion began piecing together the timeline, speaking methodically as he laid out their known facts.

"Here's what we know about the night of Lydia's murder," Dion began, his voice steady but strained. "Lydia was getting ready for the high-profile business dinner. She had an argument with someone in her penthouse. The hidden camera footage shows the beginning of this confrontation, but it's tampered with, and we're missing the crucial parts."

Stevens nodded, flipping through his notes. "The argument was likely about the blackmail scheme. Lydia had evidence that could ruin Clara's career and reputation. Clara had a lot to lose, and so did Gregory and Martin. Each of them had a reason to be desperate, but their alibis are solid."

Dion pointed to a forensic report on the table. "According to the coroner, Lydia's body showed signs of a struggle. Bruising on her wrists and arms suggests she tried to defend herself. The argument got physical, escalating beyond mere words."

Stevens interjected, "And the fatal wound was a single stab to the abdomen. The blade punctured a vital artery, causing her to bleed out quickly. There was very little time for her to call for help."

Dion's eyes narrowed as he looked over the crime scene photos again. "Here's where it gets even murkier. The scene was staged. The knife was planted in a position that doesn't make sense for it to have been dropped. And the white carpet in the living room had minimal blood stains, indicating that someone cleaned up after the fact."

Stevens added, "The forensic team found traces of bleach around the area. The killer went to great lengths to cover their tracks, which suggests premeditation. They tried to make it look like a domestic dispute that escalated, but the staging was too precise in some places and too careless in others."

Dion sighed, rubbing his temples. "It's maddening. All the suspects have airtight alibis, yet someone went to great lengths to stage the scene and plant false evidence. It feels like we're missing a key piece of the puzzle."

The tension in the room was palpable. Dion's frustration was evident as he slammed his hand on the table, causing a few papers to flutter to the floor. "We're back to where we started, and it's driving me insane. We need a breakthrough, something that ties all these loose ends together."

Stevens placed a calming hand on Dion's shoulder. "Let's take a break. We've been at this for hours. Maybe a change of scenery will help clear our heads. How about we go grab a coffee?"

Dion nodded reluctantly, knowing that stepping away might indeed help them gain a new perspective. They left the boardroom, the evidence spread out like a map of their frustration, and walked through the now-bustling police station. The morning shift had started, bringing new energy into the building, but Dion and Stevens were running on fumes.

Detective Dion and Officer Stevens left the police station, the chill of the morning air providing a brief reprieve from the suffocating weight of the case. They walked in silence to their now seemingly favorite coffee shop just down the road, the same place where they had pieced together fragments of the mystery over countless cups of coffee.

The café's familiar warmth embraced them as they stepped inside. They ordered the same drinks as last time, Dion, a strong black coffee, and Stevens, a Vanilla oat-milk latte with extra cream. The barista, recognizing them, gave a nod of acknowledgment as she prepared their drinks. The rich aroma of freshly brewed coffee filled the air, a temporary solace from the turmoil of their investigation.

They found their usual spot by the window, where the morning light cast a gentle glow across their table. Dion stared out the window, his expression a mask of frustration and contemplation. Stevens watched him for a moment before breaking the silence.

"Dion, I've noticed this case is really getting to you. More than usual. What's going on?"

For a moment, Stevens thought he wouldn't respond, but the weight of the silence was palpable. Dion's shoulders seemed to slump slightly as he took a deep breath, turning slowly to face his colleague. There was a rare vulnerability in his eyes, a reflection of emotions usually masked by his professional facade.

"You know, Stevens," Dion began, his voice softer than usual, "I usually keep my personal life separate from the job. It's easier that way. But this case... it's hitting close to home." His eyes flickered with a mix of pain and reflection, the weight of his memories pressing heavily on him.

Stevens leaned in, his curiosity piqued. "How so?"

Dion hesitated, searching for the right words. His gaze fell to his hands, gripping the edge of the table as if it might anchor him in the turbulent sea of his emotions. "Years ago, when I was just starting out as a detective, I worked a case that was eerily similar to this one. A woman was found murdered in her apartment, the scene staged to mislead us. It was my first big case, and I was determined to solve it."

He paused, his expression darkening with the weight of the memories. "I got too close, let my emotions cloud my judgment. I missed a crucial piece of evidence, and the killer walked free. A few months later, he struck again. Another woman died because I couldn't put the pieces together in time." Dion's voice wavered as he continued, each word carrying the burden of regret and guilt. "It was a devastating blow, not just to the victims and their families, but to me. I had been so sure, so confident in my approach, but my oversight had tragic consequences. The guilt has haunted me ever since."

He looked out the window again, his eyes distant. "Every time I come across a case with similar elements, it dredges up those old fears and failures. I start second-guessing every decision, wondering if I'm missing something crucial. I can't afford to make the same mistakes again."

Stevens listened intently, the gravity of Dion's words sinking in. "I had no idea, Dion. That must have been tough."

"It was," Dion admitted, his voice heavy with regret. "I promised myself I'd never let it happen again. But this case... the similarities are haunting. The blackmail, the staging, the suspects with seemingly perfect alibis. It's like I'm being tested all over again."

Stevens reached out, placing a reassuring hand on Dion's arm. "You're a great detective, Dion. We'll solve this together. You're not alone in this."

Dion managed a small, appreciative smile. Stevens sipped his coffee thoughtfully, then asked, "Dion, what was the piece of evidence you missed last time? The one that let the killer walk free?"

Dion's eyes darkened, and he seemed to retreat inward, his face etched with a mixture of pain and regret. His jaw tightened, and for a moment, it looked like he might cry, the raw emotion of the memory clawing its way to the surface. He opened his mouth to speak but no words came out. Instead, he swallowed hard and looked away, blinking rapidly.

"It doesn't matter now," he finally said, his voice barely above a whisper. "What matters is that we don't miss anything this time."

Stevens nodded, sensing the depth of Dion's turmoil and choosing not to press further. They both took a moment to compose themselves, the weight of unspoken words hanging heavily between them. The café's gentle hum provided a semblance of normalcy, a brief pause in the relentless pursuit of justice.

Just as they were finishing their toasty drinks, a young police officer burst into the café, nearly toppling a few chairs in his frantic entrance. His face was flushed with urgency, and he barely managed to catch his breath as he spoke. "Detective Knight! Officer Stevens! You need to come back to the station immediately. The footage has been recovered, and you're gonna wanna see it."

Dion and Stevens exchanged a look of immediate concern, their previous relaxation giving way to a sudden burst of adrenaline. The officer's breathless announcement and the look of panic in his eyes spoke volumes about the importance of the discovery. They quickly abandoned their half-finished coffees, their chairs scraping loudly against the tiled floor as they stood up. The air in the café, once filled with the comforting aroma of freshly brewed coffee, now seemed charged with a palpable tension.

The hurried footsteps of Dion and Stevens echoed down the street as they made their way back to the station. The sense of urgency was almost tangible, propelling them forward with a brisk pace. Each step seemed to heighten the anticipation of what awaited them back at the station. Dion's mind raced with questions, trying to piece together the implications of the newly recovered footage. The shadows of doubt that had lingered over the case seemed to shift, promising answers that might clarify the tangled web they had been unraveling.

As they reached the station, their faces set with determination, they were met by the same young officer who led them to the tech room. The bustling noise of the station seemed to fade into the background as they entered the room, their focus entirely on the task at hand.

The Missing Moment

Back at the police station, the atmosphere buzzed with anticipation. Detective Dion Knight and Officer Stevens moved swiftly through the bustling corridors, the young officer leading them to the tech department. The urgency of the recovered footage crackled in the air, bringing a sense of purpose to their steps.

They entered the room, where the only light seeped through the slatted blinds, casting thin lines of brightness against the walls. The room was filled with the quiet hum of computers and the occasional click of a mouse. A team of technicians worked intently at their stations, the glow from their monitors illuminating their faces in shades of blue and green, giving them an almost spectral appearance.

The air was thick with concentration, a faint scent of stale coffee lingering from the long hours spent on the task. Wires snaked across the floor, connecting various pieces of high-tech equipment, creating a maze-like network of technology. At the center of the room was a large monitor, the focal point of everyone's attention, paused on a grainy still image from the hidden camera footage.

Lewis, the lead technician, stood closest to the screen. His desk was cluttered with notebooks, coffee cups, and electronic gadgets. He adjusted his glasses, their lenses reflecting the frozen image, and beckoned Dion and Stevens over. Around him, other technicians whispered to each other, pointing at their screens and scribbling notes, their faces tense with the pressure of the task at hand.

"Detective, Officer, over here," called the bespectacled man named Lewis. He gestured to the large screen. "We managed to recover most of the footage, but some segments were heavily corrupted. We're still working on piecing those parts together."

Dion nodded, his heart pounding in his chest. "Show us what you have so far."

Lewis hit play, and the screen flickered to life. The footage wobbled initially, as though the camera were adjusting, but soon it stabilized, revealing a clear view of Lydia Harper's elegant penthouse. Lydia appeared in the frame, visibly agitated, pacing back and forth in front of her vanity. Her movements were restless, her gestures sharp. She was speaking, her lips moving rapidly, but the audio was garbled, rendering her words indistinct. Her frustration and anxiety were palpable, even without understanding her exact words.

"Enhance the audio," Dion instructed, his eyes fixed on the screen.

Lewis adjusted a few settings, and the audio cleared slightly. Lydia's voice, though still muffled, became more discernible. She was arguing with someone off-camera, her tone a mix of anger and desperation.

"...can't believe you did this... jeopardized everything..."

The argument grew more heated, and then a shadowy figure stepped into the frame. The figure's face was obscured, but their posture was unmistakably menacing. Tall and broad-shouldered, the person moved with a predatory grace, exuding an air of cold, calculated menace. The way they held themselves, calm and collected despite the escalating tension, suggested a professional who had done this before. Lydia recoiled, her eyes wide with fear, her hand raised defensively. The figure advanced with measured steps, their aggression controlled and deliberate, further confirming their lethal expertise.

"Who is that?" Stevens asked, leaning in closer.

"We're still trying to enhance the image," Lewis replied. "It's difficult, but we're making progress."

The argument escalated, the shadowy figure gesturing wildly. Lydia stood her ground, her face set with determination. Suddenly, the figure lunged at her, and the screen fizzled, the image distorting before cutting to black.

"Damn it," Dion muttered, frustration etching his features. "What happened to the rest?"

"We're working on it," Lewis said. "The data is heavily corrupted, but we're hopeful we can restore more of it."

Dion clenched his fists, the weight of the case pressing down on him. "We need that footage, Lewis. It's the key to everything."

Just then, Officer Stevens' phone buzzed. He glanced at the screen and his eyes widened. "Dion, I've just got confirmation on Clara's alibi. She was indeed at the business dinner that night, and several witnesses can corroborate her presence."

As they waited for the tech team to work their magic, Dion and Stevens returned to the boardroom. The large table was covered with every piece of evidence they had gathered so far. Crime scene photos, forensic reports, alibi statements, all meticulously laid out.

Dion traced a finger over the timeline they had constructed. "The argument happened while Lydia was getting ready for dinner. She was supposed to be there, but she never showed up. Someone came to her apartment, confronted her, and it turned violent."

Stevens nodded, picking up a crime scene photo. "The forensic report showed signs of a struggle. Lydia had defensive wounds on her arms and bruising on her wrists. She fought back."

Dion's eyes fell on a picture of the white carpet, almost pristine except for a few faint stains. "The killer cleaned up afterward, using bleach. They wanted to erase any trace of what happened."

Dion sighed, rubbing his temples. "We're missing something. Something crucial. The footage might give us that, but we need to keep digging."

Suddenly, a burst of sound erupted from the adjacent room, startling them. The previously muted footage now blared with clarity, the audio unmistakably clear. They heard Lydia's voice, sharp and defiant, shouting, "I'm not giving him anything in the divorce!"

Dion and Stevens exchanged a quick, alarmed glance before rushing to the tech room. The technicians were huddled around the monitor, their faces illuminated by the stark light of the screen. The room buzzed with excitement and tension as the team had managed to decode the crucial audio.

Lewis looked up as they entered, motioning for them to come closer. "We got the audio, Detective. You need to hear this."

On the screen, the footage continued. Lydia stood firm, her voice unwavering despite the fear in her eyes. The shadowy figure's presence was more ominous with the audio restored. The killer's voice was calm and chillingly detached, a stark contrast to Lydia's desperation.

"I don't care about your divorce," the figure said, their voice low and menacing. "This isn't about money. You've made powerful enemies, Lydia."

Lydia's eyes darted around the room, searching for an escape that wasn't there. "You can't scare me. I won't back down."

The killer stepped closer, their movements deliberate and measured. "You don't understand. This is bigger than you. It's about sending a message."

A tense silence filled the room as the killer's words hung in the air.

Then, the figure lunged at Lydia. The screen fizzled briefly, but the audio continued. The sounds of a struggle ensued, Lydia's desperate cries, the heavy breaths of the assailant, the sickening thud of a blow landing.

Stevens leaned in, his face etched with concentration. "That voice… we need to identify it."

Dion nodded, his mind racing. "This changes everything. Lydia wasn't just a victim of a domestic dispute. She was targeted for a reason."

Lewis paused the footage, the final frame showing Lydia's horrified expression. "We're working on enhancing the image of the assailant. This audio gives us a new direction."

Dion took a deep breath, the pieces of the puzzle finally beginning to align. "Send this to the lab for voice analysis. We need to match it to anyone in our database. And keep working on that image. We need to see who this professional is."

As they left the tech room, Dion felt a renewed sense of urgency. "We need to re-interview everyone. This wasn't just a crime of passion, it was a calculated move. Someone paid for this hit, and we need to find out who."

Stevens nodded, determination in his eyes. "Let's start with Clara Sullivan. She has the most to lose and the resources to hire a professional."

The air in the police station crackled with tension as Detective Dion Knight and Officer Stevens prepared for their next move. The revelation from the footage had shifted the case into a new, more dangerous gear. Lydia Harper's murder was no longer just a high-profile case; it was a chilling reminder of how calculated and cold-blooded human nature could be.

Dion and Stevens entered the boardroom, where their notes and evidence were still spread out on the table. The room was dimly lit by the overhead lights, casting long shadows that seemed to mimic their own sense of foreboding. Dion was already running through the implications in his mind, his thoughts racing as they prepared to confront Clara Sullivan.

"Clara's been dodging our questions," Dion said, his voice low and resolute. "We need to confront her with the new evidence. She needs to know we're not backing down."

Stevens nodded, his face set with determination. "I'll handle the questioning. You'll be there to back me up."

They traveled across town, navigating the bustling streets as the evening light cast long shadows. The police station receded in their wake as they approached a sleek, high-rise building where Clara Sullivan's office was located. Entering the building, they were greeted by the hum of modernity, marble floors, polished glass, and the soft murmur of office life coming to a close.

The elevator ride to the top floor was a silent ascent, both Dion and Stevens lost in thought. As the doors slid open, they stepped into a sleek, contemporary lobby, the design minimalistic yet elegant. The hallway leading to Clara's office was lined with dark wood paneling and modern art, a stark contrast to the weight of the confrontation awaiting them.

Clara's office was at the end of the hall, a floor-to-ceiling glass suite offering a panoramic view of the city skyline. The setting sun bathed the room in a warm, golden glow, casting a striking juxtaposition to the gravity of their mission. The golden light streaming through the glass was beautiful, but it did little to ease the tension that thickened in the air. As they approached her office, Dion felt the burden of the case settle heavily on his shoulders. This was the pivotal moment, the point where the case could either unravel or snap into place with newfound clarity.

They knocked on the door, and Clara's voice, cool and composed, called them in. She was seated behind her polished mahogany desk, her posture rigid and professional. Her eyes met theirs with a steely gaze, though there was a flicker of unease as they entered.

"Detective Knight, Officer Stevens," Clara greeted, her voice smooth but betraying a hint of apprehension. "What brings you here?"

Dion took the lead, his tone direct and unyielding. "Clara, we've made significant progress in the investigation. We've recovered crucial footage and audio that implicates someone very skilled, someone who had a personal motive and the means to hire a professional."

Clara's face remained a mask of controlled composure, but Dion could see her knuckles whiten as she gripped the edge of her desk. "I'm aware of the developments. Is there something specific you need from me?"

Stevens stepped forward, placing a folder on the desk. "This is a transcript of the newly recovered footage. It includes a confrontation between Lydia and a professional killer. The killer's voice was cold, methodical. We need to know if you recognize it or if you have any information that could help us identify them."

Clara's eyes darted briefly to the folder before returning to meet Dion's gaze. "I don't know what you're implying. I had no reason to harm Lydia. I was only trying to protect my business interests."

Dion leaned in, his voice low but forceful. "Clara, we know about the blackmail scheme Lydia had against you. She was threatening to expose you unless you paid her off. You had a clear motive. But what's more troubling is that the footage shows a professional, someone with experience in executing hits. Did you hire someone to deal with Lydia?"

Clara's face went pale, her composure cracking. "That's preposterous. I didn't hire anyone. Lydia's threats were inconvenient, but I wouldn't resort to murder."

Stevens pressed on, his tone unwavering. "We also know you were at the high-profile dinner that night. Witnesses confirm your alibi. But Lydia was supposed to be there too. She never showed up. Who could have known she would be alone?"

Clara's breathing grew rapid, her fingers tapping nervously on the desk. "I don't know what you're trying to say. I had no control over her actions. The dinner was a public event, and Lydia's absence was a personal matter."

Dion's gaze was unrelenting. "Then why does the footage indicate a premeditated plan involving someone with professional skills? If it wasn't you, then who? And why?"

Clara's defenses began to crumble. Her face flushed with a mix of anger and fear. "Fine! I admit I was angry. Lydia's blackmailing was unbearable. I might have mentioned it to someone who could deal with her. But I never expected it to go this far. I thought it would be a scare tactic, not a murder!"

Dion's heart pounded. "Who did you contact, Clara? We need names, now."

Clara's eyes filled with tears, and she broke down. "I don't know their names. I used a middleman, someone I thought I could trust. I just wanted Lydia to stop."

Her sobs became choked as she slumped forward, her hands trembling. Dion and Stevens exchanged a glance, knowing this was their moment to push for the full truth. Stevens took a step closer, his voice gentle but firm. "Clara, you need to tell us everything. The blackmail, the middleman, it's not adding up unless you give us more."

Clara's sobs gradually subsided, and she lifted her tear-streaked face, her expression a mixture of shame and resignation. "Lydia... she wasn't just blackmailing me. She was bragging about her affair with Martin. She mentioned it casually, like it was nothing. I found out about it weeks ago."

Dion leaned in, his eyes narrowing with intense focus. "So, you knew about the affair?"

"Yes," Clara replied, her voice barely a whisper. "Lydia was flaunting it, trying to belittle me. She said it was her way of getting back at me for trying to undermine her, for wanting to protect my business from her interference. I told Gregory about it, hoping it would disrupt her work. I never thought it would escalate like this."

Stevens interjected, trying to piece together the motive. "You hoped Gregory would use the affair to hurt Lydia's credibility or distract her from her blackmail schemes?"

"Yes," Clara admitted, her voice quivering. "I thought it might make her less focused, maybe even cause some personal turmoil for her. I was desperate to get her to stop meddling in our business affairs. But I never imagined it would lead to murder. I thought it would just be a way to force her to back off, to make her realize she was pushing too far."

Dion's mind raced. "Clara, did you ever directly threaten Lydia or suggest any action that could have pushed someone to violence?"

"No, no!" Clara's voice was a frantic plea. "I never threatened her. I was only trying to protect my company. I never intended for any of this to happen. I'm afraid I might have set off a chain of events I couldn't control."

The weight of Clara's confession hung heavy in the room. Dion knew that while Clara's admission explained her motive and her indirect involvement, it was clear Clara didn't orchestrate it. Perhaps fueled by jealousy, rage, there's only one person upon hearing the news that could act.

As Clara's confession settled heavily in the room, Dion and Stevens exchanged a determined glance. The pieces of the puzzle were falling into place, and a glaring truth emerged: Gregory was the one with the strongest motive. His desire to restore his lavish lifestyle and his knowledge of the affair had made him the most likely suspect.

With a sense of urgency, they quickly left Clara's office and made their way back to their unmarked car parked discreetly on the street. The city lights cast long shadows as they sped off, Dion's grip on the steering wheel tightening with each passing second.

Stevens pulled out his phone and dialed the number for their police team. "We need immediate assistance. Gregory Harper is our prime suspect. We have to locate him before he disappears."

As Stevens relayed the details, Dion focused on the road, weaving through the bustling streets with a sense of urgency. The revelation of Gregory's motive had shifted the investigation into high gear, and they knew that time was of the essence. The pressure was mounting, and they were determined to bring Gregory to justice before he could escape or destroy any remaining evidence.

Confession

The highway stretched out before them, a ribbon of asphalt winding through the encroaching darkness. Gregory Harper's car, a sleek black sedan, had been spotted heading north, slipping further away from the city with each passing minute. Dion and Stevens, now locked into the chase, were already weaving through the dense evening traffic in their unmarked vehicle, urgency palpable in every maneuver.

The late evening sky had deepened into a profound indigo, punctuated by the first flickers of starlight, their cold glow reflecting the tension inside the car. The highway's lights blurred into a streaky haze as Dion pushed the engine to its limits, the vehicle's roar cutting through the ambient hum of the highway. Every second counted, and Dion could feel the weight of the moment bearing down on him. His heart pounded in sync with the revving engine, the chase a blur of speed and focus.

Stevens, sitting beside him, was a bundle of concentrated energy, his eyes darting ahead and scanning the horizon. His fingers hovered over the radio, ready to dispatch orders to the police team. "Gregory's heading out of our jurisdiction fast," Stevens said, his voice tight with both urgency and apprehension. "We need to intercept him before he crosses into the next county. The longer we wait, the harder it will be to catch him."

Dion's knuckles whitened as he tightened his grip on the steering wheel, his face set in a determined scowl. "Push harder, Stevens. If we let him slip away now, we might never get another chance. I want roadblocks set up ahead immediately. Coordinate with the other units and make sure they're in place before we reach the county line."

The unmarked car swerved through traffic with a precision born from countless high-stakes pursuits, Dion's eyes fixed on the road ahead, his mind racing with strategies. The urgency was a tangible force in the vehicle, heightening their senses and sharpening their focus. Each mile they covered brought them closer to Gregory, but also increased the risk of losing him entirely. The chase had become a relentless race against time, each moment driving home the critical need to capture their suspect before he vanished into the night.

The highway wound through darkened fields and sparse roadside lights, creating a sense of isolation and urgency. Gregory's sedan was visible in the distance, its headlights cutting through the night like a beacon. Dion kept a steady gaze on the taillights, determined not to let the suspect out of sight.

The police radio crackled to life as Stevens relayed their location and status. "We're closing in on him, but he's not slowing down. Need backup and roadblocks on Route 23 immediately."

The static-laden response from dispatch confirmed that their request was being processed. Dion's focus remained unyielding, his eyes flickering between the road and the glowing lights of Gregory's car. The pursuit was a tense ballet of speed and strategy, the city's distant glow a stark reminder of what was at stake.

As they barreled down the highway, the terrain ahead shifted into a stretch with fewer exits and dwindling traffic. The sky above had turned an even darker shade of indigo, broken only by the harsh glare of the highway lights. Dion's eyes were locked on Gregory's car, now visibly swerving with increasing desperation. It was clear that Gregory was struggling to maintain control, his erratic driving a telltale sign of his growing panic.

The chase had reached a critical juncture, and Dion's every move was crucial. The night air was charged with the electricity of their pursuit, a tangible sense of urgency permeating the vehicle. Dion's grip on the steering wheel tightened as he leaned into a sharp turn, the unmarked car responding with agile precision. He could feel the adrenaline coursing through him, heightening his senses and sharpening his focus.

The gap between their car and Gregory's sedan narrowed rapidly. Dion's heart pounded in his chest as he executed a strategic maneuver, sliding the unmarked car into a position that would force Gregory to confront the reality of being cornered. The engine roared in protest as Dion accelerated, closing the distance with relentless determination.

Gregory's car began to slow, the driver's panic clear from the wild, jerky movements. Dion's eyes were steely, his mind working in overdrive as he assessed the situation. With a precise and practiced motion, he swung their car in front of Gregory's sedan. The abruptness of the move forced Gregory to slam on the brakes, the tires screeching in a high-pitched protest that pierced the quiet night.

The jarring impact of the brakes was a cacophony of sound that reverberated through the cool night air, followed by the grinding halt of Gregory's car. The vehicle came to a shuddering stop, its tires skidding slightly before settling. The tension was almost palpable as Dion and Stevens leaped from their car, their movements sharp and purposeful. The weight of their mission hung heavily in the air, their determination etched into every step they took.

Dion's badge glinted briefly under the harsh glare of the headlights as he approached Gregory's sedan. Each step was driven by the gravity of their objective and the urgency of the situation. The surrounding darkness seemed to close in around them, amplifying the intensity of the confrontation. As they drew closer, the night seemed to hold its breath, the outcome of this high-stakes chase hanging in the balance.

"Get out of the car, Gregory Harper!" Dion shouted, his voice carrying a commanding authority.

Gregory's face was a mask of fear and resignation as he slowly emerged from the vehicle. His hands were raised, trembling slightly as he complied. Dion and Stevens moved with practiced efficiency, each movement a testament to their training and resolve. Dion kept his eyes on Gregory, while Stevens quickly reached for the cuffs.

With a swift, practiced motion, Stevens secured the cuffs around Gregory's wrists, the click of the metal echoing in the quiet of the night. Dion's gaze remained fixed on Gregory, reading the man's demeanor. The fear was evident, but so was the resignation of someone who knew the game was up.

"You're under arrest for the murder of Lydia Harper," Dion said, his tone flat and professional. "Anything you say can and will be used against you in a court of law."

Gregory's eyes flickered with a mix of defiance and despair. "I didn't mean for it to end like this," he muttered, his voice barely audible over the hum of the night. "I only wanted her out of my life."

Stevens guided Gregory to the back of their car, the surroundings punctuated by the flashing lights of the police vehicles and the distant hum of traffic. The backup officers had arrived, their presence reinforcing the sense of resolution to the night's events.

As Gregory was placed into the back of the squad car, Dion took a deep breath, the adrenaline of the chase giving way to the gravity of their success. The pursuit had ended, but the case was not yet fully resolved. There were still questions to answer and a courtroom where the full truth would be laid bare.

Dion and Stevens stood beside their squad car, taking a moment to assess the damage. The front bumper was hanging precariously, a testament to the intensity of the chase. The right headlight was shattered, and the vehicle's sleek lines were marred by fresh dents and scrapes.

Stevens ran a hand through his hair, shaking his head with a wry smile. "Looks like we'll be driving a loaner for a while."

Dion chuckled, though his exhaustion was evident. "Yeah, but we got him. That's what matters."

The scene around them was teeming with activity. Multiple squad cars had arrived, their red and blue lights flashing in a dizzying display. Officers were everywhere, securing the area and ensuring that Gregory's vehicle was properly recovered. The road was closed off, yellow police tape cordoning off the scene to keep onlookers at bay.

Detective Knight watched as officers worked methodically, cataloging evidence and documenting the scene. He could hear snippets of conversations, orders being given, updates being shared, and the occasional murmur of disbelief at the dramatic conclusion of the chase.

"Detective Knight," an officer called out, approaching with a clipboard in hand. "We're getting ready to tow Gregory's car. Found some interesting stuff inside that might be useful for the case."

Dion nodded, his mind already shifting to the next steps. "Good work. Make sure everything is logged properly. We need to build an airtight case."

Stevens leaned against the damaged squad car, his expression a mix of relief and pride. "We did it, Dion. It's not over yet, but this is a big win."

Dion breathed a sigh of relief, the weight of the chase lifting slightly. "Yeah, it is. We're getting closer to justice for Lydia. We just need to keep pushing, keep following the evidence."

As the chaos of the scene continued around them, Dion took a moment to appreciate the efforts of everyone involved. The officers, the technicians, and his partner Stevens, all had played a crucial role in bringing Gregory to justice. The road to the courtroom would be long, but for now, they could take solace in the fact that they had made a significant breakthrough. There was one thing to do; a final interview.

The interview room was stark and utilitarian, its white walls and fluorescent lights casting a harsh, unflattering glow over the small space. Gregory Harper sat at the metal table, his wrists cuffed and his posture slumped in defeat. His once sharp, well-tailored suit now seemed disheveled and ill-fitting, a visual testament to the unraveling of his carefully maintained facade.

Detective Dion entered the room, his expression a mix of professionalism and solemnity. He took a seat across from Gregory, his demeanor calm but resolute. Stevens, standing by the door, remained silent, letting Dion lead the questioning.

"Gregory," Dion began, his voice steady and controlled, "we have all the evidence we need. It's time for you to tell us the truth. Why did you kill Lydia Harper?"

Gregory's eyes were red-rimmed and glassy, his face etched with the weariness of someone who had reached the breaking point. He took a deep, shuddering breath, his shoulders shaking as the weight of his actions seemed to crush him.

"I… I didn't mean for any of this," Gregory said, his voice trembling. "I found out about the affair right in the middle of our divorce from Clara.. She was taking everything from me, my life, my reputation, everything I had worked for."

Tears began to well up in Gregory's eyes, and he looked away, unable to meet Dion's steady gaze. "I wanted to get back at her. I wanted her to suffer, to feel the pain she was causing me. I hired someone to make her disappear. I thought… I thought it would fix everything. I wanted my life back, the life she took away from me."

His voice broke as he continued, his confession coming out in ragged gasps. "I didn't realize how far things would go. I didn't understand the gravity of what I was doing until now. I'm so sorry. I never meant for it to end like this."

Gregory's tears fell freely now, streaming down his cheeks as he sobbed uncontrollably. The harsh reality of his actions seemed to overwhelm him, his cries echoing in the sterile room. Dion watched in silence, his own emotions carefully controlled. The confession was a confirmation of the case's resolution, but it was also a reminder of the tragic consequences of desperation and betrayal.

"Thank you for your confession, Gregory," Dion said softly, though his tone remained firm. "You'll have the chance to explain yourself further in court. For now, you'll be processed and held accountable for your actions."

As Dion stood to leave, Stevens moved forward to take over, preparing to escort Gregory to the next phase of the legal process. The weight of the case, the emotions, and the revelations were all heavy, but for now, justice had been served.

Detective Dion and Officer Stevens emerged from the interview room, their faces reflecting the gravity of the night's events. The air in the police station felt thick with the culmination of their relentless investigation. As they made their way back to their desks, a sense of weary accomplishment settled between them. Gregory's confession had brought clarity to the case, but there was still a lingering need to ensure all the pieces were in place.

Just as they were about to sit down and discuss their next steps, Lewis, the technician who had been working tirelessly to restore the hidden camera footage, approached them with a sense of urgency.

"Detective Dion, Officer Stevens," Lewis said, his face illuminated by the glow of his laptop screen. "We've managed to recover one last piece of footage that might be crucial. You need to see this."

Dion and Stevens exchanged a look of intrigue and followed Lewis back to the tech room. The room, bathed in the eerie glow of computer screens and dimmed lights, had an air of quiet anticipation. The technicians, their faces etched with exhaustion, had gathered around a large monitor in the center of the room. The screen flickered as the final piece of footage was prepared for viewing.

Lewis hit play, and the footage began to roll. The image was still grainy but much clearer than before. It showed the interior of Lydia Harper's penthouse, the scene now eerily familiar from earlier footage. The timestamp indicated it was shortly after Lydia's murder.

The camera's view was fixed on the entrance of the penthouse, the door opening with a soft creak. Gregory Harper appeared in the frame, his demeanor tense and hurried. He moved cautiously, his eyes darting around as if ensuring no one was watching. The room was dimly lit, the shadows elongating as he moved.

Gregory's movements were deliberate and calculated as he approached the crime scene. The footage showed him bending down to retrieve something from his coat, a familiar object. Dion's heart raced as the realization dawned. Gregory was holding the very knife that had been planted at the scene.

With a furtive glance around, Gregory placed the knife on a side table near the body, adjusting its position as if arranging a misplaced item. He then turned and quickly exited the penthouse, the door closing behind him with a soft click. The footage ended with the image of the knife, a damning piece of evidence, resting on the table, a chilling testament to Gregory's attempt to stage the crime scene.

The room fell into a heavy silence as the footage concluded. Dion and Stevens stood motionless, absorbing the gravity of the revelation they had just witnessed. The dim light from the projector cast long shadows on the walls, reflecting the seriousness of the moment. The final piece of evidence had conclusively tied Gregory to the crime scene, not merely as the mastermind but as an active participant in manipulating the investigation.

"Well, that confirms it," Stevens said, breaking the silence with a voice tinged with relief and awe. "Gregory wasn't just the mastermind; he actively tried to cover his tracks by planting the knife. This is the final proof we needed."

Dion, still processing the weight of the evidence, nodded slowly. His face, usually stern and impassive, softened with a mixture of grim satisfaction and profound relief. "It's over now. We have everything we need to secure a conviction. Gregory's attempt to frame Martin was a desperate move, but it was all for nothing. The truth is out."

As they left the tech room, the palpable tension that had gripped them for weeks seemed to lift, replaced by an overwhelming sense of closure. Dion and Stevens exchanged a look of quiet triumph, the burden of the investigation finally lifting from their shoulders. They walked through the corridors of the precinct, their footsteps echoing softly against the walls, a subtle, rhythmic reminder of the case's conclusion.

The weight of the high-profile case had been immense, a pressure that had tested their limits and pushed them to their professional edges. Yet, in this moment of quiet relief, there was an unmistakable sense of achievement. The resolution of the case marked a return to order and integrity in their world of crime and investigation. As they reached the exit, Dion took a deep breath, allowing himself a rare moment of contemplation and relief. The final act in this complex drama had been played, and the resolution, though bittersweet, signified not just the end of a case but a reaffirmation of their commitment to justice.

A Detective's Reflection

The following morning arrived with a muted, overcast sky, casting a somber light over the city. The usual hustle and bustle of the urban landscape seemed subdued, as if the city itself was taking a moment to reflect on the conclusion of the high-profile Lydia Harper case. Detective Dion Knight walked towards the police station with a determined stride, the weight of the past few days heavy on his shoulders. The recent resolution of the case, while a significant achievement, had left him physically and emotionally drained. The cool, damp air seemed to mirror his mood, adding a layer of melancholy to the gray morning.

As he approached the entrance, Dion was met by a throng of news crews camped outside the police station. Their presence was a stark reminder of the media frenzy that had accompanied the case from the beginning. Photographers clicked away furiously, their cameras flashing intermittently as they vied for a shot of the detective. A reporter, holding a microphone with the station's logo prominently displayed, called out to him with practiced eagerness.

"Detective Knight! How did you manage to solve the Lydia Harper case? What was the key breakthrough?"

Dion paused for a moment, his gaze fixed on the reporter with a mixture of exhaustion and determination. The question hung in the air, but he offered no response. After a beat of silence, Dion turned and walked past the reporters, his expression set in a resolute line. He pushed through the glass doors of the station and entered the familiar confines of the building, seeking refuge from the prying eyes of the press.

Inside, the station buzzed with the usual activity. Officers and detectives moved purposefully through the corridors, their conversations a low murmur against the backdrop of clacking keyboards and ringing phones. Dion made his way to his desk, where Officer Stevens was already waiting. Despite the long hours and relentless pace of the investigation, Stevens seemed energized and eager, his enthusiasm a stark contrast to Dion's weary demeanor.

"Morning, Dion!" Stevens greeted with a broad grin. "Can you believe it? We actually nailed it! I've been going over everything, and it feels like a weight has been lifted."

Dion managed a tired smile, acknowledging his partner's excitement. "Yeah, it feels good to have it wrapped up. But we've still got the final debrief with Chief Constable Harris."

As if on cue, the call came through. The Chief Constable's office wanted them to report immediately. Dion and Stevens exchanged a final look, a silent understanding passing between them. They both knew that the briefing was the last step in closing out the case officially.

As they entered the office, the familiar, heavy scent of vape smoke greeted them. Chief Constable Harris was seated behind his desk, grappling with yet another new vape flavor. The room was hazy with the swirling clouds of burnt toffee, and Harris was mid-cough, his face reddened as he tried to clear his lungs from the unexpected intensity of the flavor.

"Blasted thing!" Harris sputtered, waving his hand in front of his face. "I swear, these vapes are worse than cigarettes. Can't find a decent flavor to save my life."

Dion and Stevens exchanged a glance, their expressions reflecting a mix of amusement and sympathy for their beleaguered superior. They took their seats across from Harris, who was still grimacing as he fumbled with the vape pen.

"Good morning, Chief," Dion said, his voice steady despite his exhaustion.

Harris managed a strained smile and set the offending vape aside. "Morning, detectives. I'd say it's been an interesting week, but I'd be lying. I've been drowning in media calls and sleepless nights. Let's get down to it."

Harris cleared his throat and turned to the folder in front of him. He shuffled through several papers before finally looking up at Dion and Stevens. "I've been briefed on the latest developments. Gregory Harper's arrest and the evidence against him have been solidified, and the media frenzy is reaching its peak. They're eager for any updates, and frankly, so am I."

Dion nodded. "The final piece of footage confirmed Gregory's involvement. We've secured his confession, and the evidence ties him directly to the crime scene. The case is essentially wrapped up."

Harris leaned back in his chair, the tension in his shoulders easing slightly. "That's good to hear. I want to extend my thanks to both of you for your hard work. This case has been a challenge, but it looks like we're finally reaching the end."

He paused, his gaze shifting between Dion and Stevens as if weighing his next words carefully. "I'm aware this case has taken its toll on all of us, especially on you two. The media has been relentless, and I can't thank you enough for holding the line. Your dedication hasn't gone unnoticed."

Stevens, always eager to contribute, leaned forward. "It's been a tough one, but the results speak for themselves. I'm just glad we were able to piece it all together. Gregory's been behind bars, but it's important to make sure justice is served correctly."

Harris nodded in agreement. "Absolutely. There's still the matter of ensuring the trial goes smoothly. I need you both to be prepared for the next phase, media briefings, court appearances, and so on. It's not over until the gavel falls."

Dion rubbed the back of his neck, his weariness evident. "Understood. We'll make sure everything is in order."

Dion and Stevens exchanged glances, the weight of their achievement evident in their expressions. They had navigated the complexities of the investigation with persistence and skill, and the sense of accomplishment was palpable. As they prepared to rise and leave the office, Harris called out one final time.

"Detectives, before you go, one more thing," Harris began, a rare smile breaking through his typically stern demeanor. "I'm pleased to announce that Officer Stevens is being promoted to Detective. Your performance on this case has been exemplary, and it's time that your hard work is officially recognized."

Stevens's eyes widened in surprise and joy. He looked at Dion, who returned the look with a proud smile. It was a well-deserved promotion, and Stevens's enthusiasm was evident in his beaming expression.

"And," Harris continued, "I'm making it official that you two will be working as equal partners from now on. Your synergy and dedication to solving this case have demonstrated that you're a formidable team. I expect great things from both of you in future investigations."

Dion nodded in acknowledgment, his weariness momentarily forgotten as he absorbed the significance of the announcement. The recognition of their partnership was both an honor and a responsibility. The collaborative effort they had shown throughout the case had forged a strong bond, and now it was being formally acknowledged.

With a final nod, Dion and Stevens left Harris's office. The conclusion of the Lydia Harper murder case was imminent, and their relentless pursuit of the truth had paved the way for justice. The city would soon be aware of the outcome, and as the detectives prepared for the final stages of the investigation, they knew that their hard work had brought a measure of closure to a deeply tragic story.

The morning's events had left Detective Dion and, now, Detective Stevens with a profound sense of relief. The media frenzy that had gripped the city was gradually subsiding, and the weight of the Lydia Harper case was lifting from their shoulders. They returned to their desks in the now-familiar, subdued atmosphere of the police station, where the air was tinged with the faint aroma of coffee and the occasional murmur of activity from their colleagues.

As they settled into their seats, the tension of the past few weeks seemed to dissipate, replaced by a quiet sense of accomplishment. Stevens, ever the more buoyant of the two, glanced over at Dion with a smile. His eyes, though tired, held a spark of genuine appreciation and camaraderie.

"Well, Dion," Stevens began, leaning back in his chair with a hint of satisfaction in his voice, "looks like we've wrapped this one up. Good work, man. You really pulled through this time."

Dion, normally reserved and stoic, allowed himself a rare moment of reflection. He ran a hand through his hair, the exhaustion evident in his eyes, but there was a subtle shift in his demeanor, a release of the stress that had weighed him down. "Thanks, Stevens. It's been a hell of a ride. I've been thinking a lot about this case and how it's affected me."

Stevens nodded, his expression growing more serious. "I know this case hit you hard. It's not just about solving the crime; it's about the personal impact it has. I've seen you wrestle with it, and I can tell it's been a struggle."

Dion sighed, the lines of worry on his face softening. "Yeah, it's been tough. I've had this one case lingering over me for a while, and I suppose it was always in the back of my mind. It's hard not to let it get to you when you're so immersed in the details."

Stevens leaned forward, his tone becoming more earnest. "You know, you've redeemed yourself in a big way. The last case, it was a rough one, and you took it hard. But this time, you got the right person. You brought justice to light, and that means something. It's not just about solving the case; it's about getting it right."

Dion gave a nod of appreciation, his gratitude evident. "I needed to hear that. It's easy to get caught up in the pressure and doubt yourself. But knowing that we did our job, that we made a difference, it's a relief."

The echoes of the case had finally stilled, replaced by a deep sense of redemption. The haunting memories of his previous high-profile failure, where an innocent man had suffered due to his haste, began to fade into the background. This time, every step had been measured, every piece of evidence meticulously examined. Gregory Harper was behind bars, and Dion was confident they had the right person. For the first time in years, the weight of his past mistakes felt lighter, replaced by the solace of justice well-served.

Their conversation naturally shifted from the intense focus of their recent work to lighter, more personal topics. Dion and Stevens walked side by side, their steps echoing softly in the corridor. The weight of their shared experience had forged a deeper bond between them, evident in the relaxed way they interacted. They chuckled over anecdotes from past cases, reminiscing about the eccentricities of their suspects and the bizarre twists that had punctuated their investigations. Each story was a thread in the rich tapestry of their careers, and today, they allowed themselves to weave these threads into a tapestry of camaraderie and mutual respect.

Dion's eyes wandered to the clock on the wall, noting the time with a hint of surprise. It was already midday, and the realization that they had a rare stretch of unstructured time brought a sense of calm. The pressures of the case had given way to a welcome pause, and Dion found himself savoring the moment of reprieve.

He turned to Stevens, who was absorbed in recounting a particularly humorous encounter with a witness.

"You know, with everything settled and no immediate tasks left," Dion began, his voice carrying a note of contemplation, "maybe we should take advantage of the break."

Stevens glanced up from his animated story, his expression shifting from amusement to curiosity. "You mean leave early?"

Dion nodded, a weary but genuine smile stretching across his face. The lines of stress that had marked his features for weeks seemed to soften, revealing a more relaxed demeanor. "Yeah. We've earned it. And besides, we should celebrate your promotion. It's not every day you get a new title."

Stevens's face lit up with a mixture of excitement and relief. The promotion, which had been a bright spot amid the relentless demands of their work, now felt even more significant as they approached the end of a challenging chapter. "That sounds like a great idea," he agreed, his enthusiasm evident. "Where do you want to go?" Stevens asked.

"Pub?" questioned Dion.

"Pub."

To celebrate, Dion and Stevens found themselves back at The Rusty Anchor in the early afternoon, the familiar atmosphere of the pub providing a sense of closure. The dim lighting and rich aroma of aged wood welcomed them like an old friend. The bartender, recognizing them, greeted them with a nod as they approached the bar.

Dion ordered his usual pint of stout, the dark, hearty beer a fitting reward for the end of a grueling case. Stevens, now officially promoted to detective, chose his favorite pink gin with lemonade, the half-strawberry garnish adding a touch of color to the occasion.

They found a vacant table in the corner, a weathered wooden structure that had seen countless stories unfold over the years. As they sat down, a sense of achievement and camaraderie hung in the air.

Dion raised his glass, his eyes meeting Stevens'. "To Detective Theodore Stevens," he said, his voice filled with pride.

Stevens beamed, lifting his own glass. "To Detective Knight, my mentor and partner. Here's to many more cases solved together."

They clinked their glasses together, the sound of celebration mingling with the low hum of the pub. As they took a sip of their drinks, savoring the moment, a sudden explosion rocked the pub, shaking the walls and sending a tremor through the floor.

Patrons gasped, and the once lively chatter turned into a cacophony of alarmed voices. Dion and Stevens instinctively dropped their glasses and bolted to their feet, their senses heightened by the unexpected blast.

"What the hell was that?" Stevens exclaimed, his eyes wide with shock.

The two detectives moved swiftly through the pub, their celebratory mood replaced by the urgency of a new crisis. The once cozy atmosphere of The Rusty Anchor was now filled with tension and uncertainty. As they pushed through the heavy wooden door and into the street, they were met with a scene of chaos, smoke was billowing from a couple of blocks away.

Dion turned to Stevens, his expression resolute. "Looks like our work isn't done yet."